MW00425129

BREAKING AWAY

DELTA FORCE STRONG BOOK #3

ELLE JAMES

TWISTED PAGE INC

BREAKING AWAY

DELTA FORCE STRONG BOOK #3

New York Times & USA Today
Bestselling Author

ELLE JAMES

Copyright © 2020 by Elle James

All rights reserved.

No part of this book may be reproduced in any form or by any electronic or mechanical means, including information storage and retrieval systems, without written permission from the author, except for the use of brief quotations in a book review.

© date Twisted Page Inc. All rights reserved.

ISBN EBOOK: 978-1-62695-339-0

ISBN PRINT: 978-1-62695-377-2

Dedicated to my editor Delilah Devlin, my proofreaders and my dogs, Bandit and Charli, who almost didn't let me make this happen. Love you all!

Elle James

AUTHOR'S NOTE

Enjoy other military books by Elle James

Delta Force Strong

Visit ellejames.com for titles and release dates
For hot cowboys, visit her alter ego Myla Jackson
at mylajackson.com
and join Elle James's Newsletter at
https://ellejames.com/contact/

CHAPTER 1

"THIS IS Kylie Adams reporting to you from the Logar Province of Afghanistan where Taliban forces have attacked an Afghan security outpost in a town only forty kilometers from the capital city of Kabul." Kylie squatted behind the remaining wall of what had once been a school in the province, talking in low, clear tones into the microphone, while staring into the video camera.

An explosion rocked the earth nearby, shaking dust loose from the jagged wall.

"Did you get that?" Kylie asked, glancing upward.

"Yeah. Can we get out of here before the

battle comes to us?" Josh Bolton, her young cameraman, cringed every time a mortar exploded nearby.

Kylie straightened and looked over the broken wall. "I want to get a little closer to the actual security building to show the damage.

"Ma'am." Sergeant Garcia, the Army Ranger assigned to escort her through the battle, pressed a hand to her shoulder. "You need to get down. Those are live rounds exploding, and those guns going off are using real bullets."

Kylie fought to keep from rolling her eyes. Just because she was a female on a battlefield, didn't mean she was an idiot. She knew the risks and didn't mind taking them to get the stories she had built her reputation on.

Because she was in excellent shape and so good at being right down in the action, showing the human side of the conflict, she had earned a spot working with the Army Rangers while they were on maneuvers. She was sure it didn't hurt that she was giving the U.S. Army Rangers some positive press on their war against terrorists.

The current mission was to extract an Afghan informant whose cover had been blown. The U.S. owed him protection, and the man had vital information about the location of one of the Taliban leaders notorious for kidnapping women and children and selling them into the sex trade.

She was going to be there for that extraction, if she had to low-crawl to the next location.

"What? Seriously? Fuck!" Garcia said behind her.

Kylie ducked below the wall and looked back at the soldier.

The man who'd told her to get down touched his hand to his helmet and tilted his head slightly. "Roger. Will do." His focus aimed at her, his lips thinning into a grim line. "Time to bug out. The point men are being overrun by bogeys. We have to get you out of here, before they get to us."

"But we haven't gotten to Faaid, your informant."

"It's my job to make sure you're safe. Besides, they didn't find him where he said he'd be. More than likely, he left when he saw it was getting hot." He jerked his head. "We need to move quickly."

Garcia herded her and Josh back the way they'd come, zigzagging through the rubble of a bombed-out village.

Shouts sounded behind them.

She heard the soldier curse behind her, and then he yelled, "Run!"

Kylie's pulse jumped. She took off, scrambling over crumbled walls, piles of brick and rubble, followed by her cameraman.

"We can't outrun them," her soldier said. "Make a left. We'll find a place to hole up until they pass."

Kylie jagged left onto a street she could actually run down without tripping over stones and brick. The buildings on either side were damaged, and appeared unoccupied, but they were fairly intact.

"On your left! That door," Sergeant Garcia barked. "Get inside."

Josh burst through the door into the building.

Kylie blew through behind him.

Shots rang out in the street.

Her heart in her throat, Kylie spun to check for the good sergeant.

She was about to go out and look for him when he fell across the threshold and tried to drag himself inside.

Kylie's heart leaped into her throat. The man had been shot in the arm and leg. He wasn't moving fast, and he couldn't hold the rifle that fell through the door with him.

"Help him," Kylie shouted to her cameraman.

Between Josh and Kylie, they dragged Sergeant Garcia into the building and slammed the door.

"They're coming," the sergeant said through gritted teeth. "I. Can't. Shoot." He grimaced as he pressed his good hand to the wound in his leg.

"We need to apply pressure to these wounds," Kylie said to her cameraman.

"You apply pressure, I'll shoot anyone coming through the door." Josh pulled off his T-shirt. "Use this."

"Bullshit." Kylie shoved the shirt back at him. "I'm a better shot, and you know it." She took the soldier's rifle from him. "Drag him back behind that wall. I'll take care of anyone coming through the door.

Josh hesitated.

She gave him a fierce frown. "You know I'm right. I grew up in Texas. I learned to fire a gun before I learned how to comb my hair." She pointed to the back of the building. "Go. Now."

Josh jumped and snagged Garcia's good hand. "Hold on tight."

The sergeant groaned as Josh dragged him across the floor into the back of the building, out of sight.

Kylie grabbed the soldier's weapon, ejected the magazine to check for rounds and slammed it back in. She had enough left to do some damage. Question was, did she have enough rounds to protect them from an army of Taliban fighters, if there were more than a few?

She found a wall to hide behind for cover and lay down in a prone position, elbows on the floor, the weapon resting lightly in her hands, her finger on the trigger guard. She sighted down the barrel at the entrance to the building and waited. With each measured breath, she calmed her wildly beating heart and focused on defending her cameraman and the soldier who'd been tasked to protect her.

"Holy shit," Josh called out.

Kylie's heartrate spiked. "What?"

"We've got company back here."

"What do you mean?" she called out as quietly as she could. "And hold it down. We don't want to give away our location.

Josh poked his head around the corner. "Faaid."

"What about him?"

"He's back here, hiding behind a pile of boxes."

"What?" Kylie glanced over her shoulder. Not like she could see into the back of the building, but seriously. The man the Rangers had been tasked with extracting was hiding in the back of an abandoned building.

He probably hadn't trusted the Americans to get him out alive and figured on getting himself out.

Until the village had been overrun by a contingent of Taliban.

A noise outside the building brought Kylie's attention back to the entrance. "Shhh," she said as loudly as she dared, hoping that Josh had heard her, but the people outside hadn't.

Footsteps pounded on the ground on the other side of the front wall. They passed.

Kylie started to let out a sigh when more feet pounded the ground outside and stopped.

Her breath lodged in her throat. The finger hovering over the trigger guard slipped onto the cool metal trigger.

She drew in a slow, steadying breath and waited, remembering her hunter education class in high school. Be sure of what you're shooting at before you pull the trigger.

The people on the other side of the door could be friendly forces.

Then again...they could be members of the Taliban. They were searching for Faaid, along with the Army Rangers. While the Rangers wanted to get him out alive, the Taliban wanted to eliminate him.

If they knew he was inside the building where Kylie, Josh and Sergeant Garcia were located, they wouldn't hesitate to storm in, take what they wanted and kill anyone who got in their way.

Where were the other soldiers? Had the Taliban killed them? Holy shit. Were they on their own?

The door slammed open.

Kylie's heart leaped into her throat. She swallowed hard to keep from letting loose a startled scream. Though her heart pounded against her ribs, she kept her hands and arms steady, her eyes trained on the man walking through the door.

Dressed all in black with a black turban, he

wasn't one of their guys. He carried an AK-47 at the ready.

A noise sounded from the rear of the building, like someone kicked a stone or dropped something on the hard floor.

Kylie winced as if she'd been stung by a bee.

The man at the door swung his rifle in Kylie's direction and fired a burst of bullets, hitting the wall above her head.

Apparently, he hadn't had the same shoot-don't-shoot training Kylie had. He was of the philosophy of shoot first, pick through the bodies later.

And he was headed her way.

Kylie trained her sights on him.

The man let loose another burst of bullets.

Kyle winced as debris from the wall rained down on her head.

If he got past her, he'd kill the others. Kylie aimed for his left chest and squeezed the trigger.

One round to the heart, and the man went down.

"Kylie?" Josh's voice called out. "You all right?"

"I'm good," she said. More footsteps pounded in the street outside the building heading their way. "But I don't know for how long." She sighted her weapon on the open door.

A shadow raced past it, and then a man in black dove through, rolled to his feet and came up shooting.

Most of Kylie's shooting experience had been with stationary targets. She aimed and fired, but the man moved so fast, Kylie missed her first shot.

The man turned toward her, his AK-47 aimed at her position.

Kylie fired again, hitting him in the chest as he pulled his trigger.

His bullet hit just above her head, showering dust and pieces of wall down on her.

Another man raced through the door with a machinegun and started firing indiscriminately.

Kylie pulled back behind her wall and lay as low to the ground as possible until the man ceased firing.

Then she poked her head and the barrel of her rifle out and fired at the man.

At the last second, he moved, and the bullet hit his arm, but not badly enough to keep him from setting off another burst of gunfire, getting closer to Kylie's location.

She ducked back and lay flat against the floor

She couldn't come out long enough to fire again, the man kept shooting short bursts.

Shouts sounded outside, and the sound of men running worried Kylie. She would run out of bullets soon, if she got another chance to fire.

The gunfire ceased, and the clang of metal hitting the floor told her the Taliban shooter was changing magazines.

If she hoped to get this guy, she needed to do it while he was vulnerable, reloading his gun.

Kylie leaned around the corner and aimed her rifle.

The shooter slammed another magazine into the machinegun.

Before he could raise it to fire, Kylie launched a bullet into the man's heart.

Four men ran through the door, all wearing the same black outfits and black turbans as the other two Kylie had nailed.

She'd been lucky the first three times. The men had come in separately. How was she going to shoot four in a row?

She aimed, fired and missed the first guy.

The Taliban men all hit the ground, making it hard for her to aim at them.

Slowly, they moved forward, inching their way toward her.

Kylie's pulse pounded in her ears. She couldn't let the fact that there were four against one get inside her head and mess with her. She had to protect Josh, Sergeant Garcia and Faaid. They were depending on her.

One of the men fired at her, hitting so close to her head, she could almost feel the buzz of the bullet zipping past her ear.

She ducked back behind the wall for a moment, dragged in a deep breath and whipped back around the corner, her rifle aiming at the last position of the closest combatant.

He wasn't there. The Taliban soldier stood over her, his AK-47 pointing down at her face.

Kylie gasped. She didn't have time to jerk her weapon up to kill the man. As she stared up at the barrel of his gun, her life passed before her eyes. The last few years as a war correspondent, before that, falling in love with the one man she'd almost given up her dreams for. He was her only regret.

Several shots were fired.

Kylie waited for the pain but felt nothing except for warm blood spraying across her face.

The man standing over her dropped his weapon, and then collapsed, landing on top of Kylie.

His weight crushed the air from her lungs. Kylie fought to get out from beneath him, but he was too heavy. Who had shot him? Was there another enemy in the building? She had to get out from under the man and be prepared to protect her team.

Suddenly, the dead Taliban man flipped over and landed on his back beside Kylie.

She scrambled to bring her weapon up in her hands and aim at the man who'd saved her life, afraid he'd only saved her because he'd wanted the Taliban soldier to die. For all she knew, he'd want her and her team to die as well.

Rolling onto her back, she aimed up at a different man staring down at her.

He held up his hands. "Whoa, little lady. You don't want to shoot your rescuer. It really destroys the whole superhero image." He winked and smiled. As he stared at her, his smile slipped. "Kylie?"

Those rugged good looks were a little more seasoned, but that voice could not be mistaken. Kylie's heart stuttered. "Mac?"

"What the hell are you doing out here in enemy territory?" he demanded, his brow descending.

Even though he'd saved her life, she bristled. "For the same reason you are."

"You came out here to shoot Taliban insurgents?" Mac shook his head. "I thought you were a journalist."

"I am," she said, pushing to a sitting position. "Things just got away from us. I had it under control." She looked away.

Mac snorted. "Under control when you were about to be shot in the head?"

She shrugged. "Well, I did...until those last four came bustin' through." Kylie sighed. "I guess I should thank you for saving my life."

"Don't sound so disappointed." He held out his hand. "And you could do a better job of saying thank you."

Her lips pressed into a thin line as she laid her hand in his.

Suddenly, she was yanked onto her feet and into his arms. He kissed her hard, his mouth claiming hers just like he had all those years ago.

And just like she had every time he'd held her

in his arms, she melted against him, her arm circling the back of his neck. She returned the kiss, hungry for him.

She could have lost herself in him forever.

"Kylie?" Josh called out. "You okay?"

Mac held onto her a moment longer, finally releasing her lips, though his arm remained around her waist.

"I'm okay," Kylie called out, her voice husky. Safe from the Taliban, but not sure she was safe from heartache.

"Is it safe to come out?" Josh called out. "Sergeant Garcia needs a medic."

"You can come out," she said and stepped away from Mac.

His jaw tightened the way it had when she'd walked away from him all those years ago. Yeah, she'd missed him, and the spark was still there on her part. Based on his kiss, he hadn't forgotten her either.

The spark was there, but had he forgiven her for choosing her career over him?

"MAC! YOU IN THERE?" a male voice called out from the outside of the building. Rucker Sloan burst through the door, his weapon ready. He aimed at Mac and Kylie until recognition dawned in his eyes. "Damn it, Mac. I thought you were a dead man when I heard all that shooting."

"I'm fine," Mac said, though his chest felt as if he'd been punched in the ribs. "Found a few of our Taliban friends about to make Swiss cheese out of one of our citizens."

Several more of his teammates entered, Sergeant Ryan "Dash" Hayes in the lead.

Dash stopped, his eyes widening, a grin spreading across his face. "Whoa, Mac, where'd you find the babe?"

Mac frowned. "She's not a babe."

"From where I'm standing, I'd say she is," Mike "Blade" Calhoun said with a flash of his bright blue eyes. He pulled his K-Bar knife out of the scabbard attached to his belt and rubbed his thumb across the blade. "You took care of all six of these guys?"

"There was a seventh man, but he got away." Mac shook his head. "I only got three of these. Miss Adams took out the first three before I arrived."

John "Tank" Sanders and Craig "Bull" Bullington turned over the three Kylie had killed.

Tank whistled. "Hey, I think we have a winner."

"What do you mean?" Mac asked.

Tank lifted his chin toward the body. "This guy looks like one of the guys on our most wanted list."

Rucker, Dash and Mac gathered around the dead man.

"Looks like Abdul Ahktar," Rucker confirmed.

"Brother of Mullah Ahktar?" Dash asked.

Tank nodded.

"Isn't Mullah Ahktar one of the bloodiest field commanders of the Taliban?" Kylie asked.

Rucker nodded. "He's not going to be happy to learn his brother was killed. Even worse...by a woman."

"Sweetheart," Dash said, "you'll have a price on your head as long as you're in the theater."

"You might want to consider leaving Afghanistan," Tank said.

"I can't leave," Kylie said, frowning. "I'm covering the war for my syndicate. They expect me to give them live-action news about the war efforts."

"Ahktar will hunt you down." Rucker said. "He's done it before. That Marine who killed

Ahktar's second in command lasted a total of five days before Ahktar's best sniper took him out."

Mac's frown deepened. "Rucker's right. Ahktar's like a bulldog with his teeth sunk deep. He won't let go. Kylie, you're not safe around here."

"I was never safe to begin with. I'll manage," Kylie said.

"You don't understand." Mac gripped her arms. "You killed his brother. Once he gets wind of his brother's death, Ahktar won't let you out of this country alive. Your best bet is to get the hell out before he learns who did the shooting. That it was a woman will make him even angrier."

Kylie's brow dipped. "I'm not going. This is my job. It's what I do. Besides, I came to get footage on the extraction and to interview Faaid." She squared her shoulders and faced Rucker, her chin rising. "Now, we should concentrate on more important matters."

"What's more important than keeping you alive?" Mac asked.

"The life of one of our soldiers. Do you have a medic with you?"

Bull lifted a finger. "That would be me."

"The Ranger I've been working with needs assistance. He has a couple of gunshot wounds. He's in the back of the building with my cameraman and the Afghan the Rangers were sent in to find and extract."

Mac's eyebrows rose. "Faaid?"

Kylie's lips twisted. "Yup. The man of the hour."

Bull hurried toward the back. Tank followed.

Mac shook his head. "We were sent in when the intelligence guys caught wind the Rangers were being set up to fail. The Taliban found out where Faaid was and got here with twice the numbers of the Ranger squad sent in to extract the informant." His lips quirked upward in a smile. "I can't say that I expected to find you holding off all those Taliban soldiers, while protecting the man everyone was after."

"I didn't plan it that way." Kylie sighed. "This was supposed to be a fairly simple extraction. Get in, rescue Faaid and get back out. Capture the action on video, conduct an interview with Faaid and show what a great job our folks in uniform are doing." She snorted softly. "Simple."

"Until it wasn't so simple." Mac nodded, glad he'd made it in time to stop the Taliban gunman from shooting the woman who'd ditched his ass all those years ago.

CHAPTER 2

KYLIE'S HEART beat fast and furious. She couldn't tell if it was from the adrenaline rush of having had to kill three Taliban terrorists or because she was standing now with the only man she'd ever loved.

She feasted her eyes on him, taking all of him in. God, he was sexy in his desert camouflage uniform and helmet. She couldn't have distinguished him from any other soldier except for the eyes and that low, resonant voice that made her blood hum and her heart sing.

One of Mac's teammates poked his head through the door of the building. "You guys need to wrap up this party. We've got incoming."

Tank emerged from the back of the building,

the Army Ranger slung over his shoulder like a sack of potatoes. "Party?" he said. "I've had about all the fun I can stand in one day. Yo, Blade, what's happening outside?"

"Dawg's on the roof," Blade said. "He'll provide cover while we make our way out of this village."

Mac held out his hand to Kylie. "Ready to blow this popsicle stand?"

She nodded.

Together, they hurried for the door.

Rucker and Dash reached it first.

"We'll provide more cover while you get your lady, the cameraman, our informant and the Ranger out."

The two men moved out and into position to defend the others.

Mac pushed Kylie behind him, stepped through the door first and looked around for any sources of trouble. Once he was convinced she was fairly safe, he turned to Kylie. "Come on."

She let him pull her down the street, taking them toward the edge of town. They ran, keeping ahead of any terrorists who might be stalking them.

"Where are we going?" Kylie asked.

Mac held her hand tightly. "Our extraction point is at the edge of town."

Tank followed, the Ranger draped over his shoulder, Faaid and Josh following close behind. Other members of Mac's team formed a semicircle around the group.

Ahead, she could see the edge of town. As they came up beside the last building, she spotted the Blackhawk helicopters, lowering to the ground.

Army Rangers were loading onto one of them. As Kylie watched, the full chopper lifted off.

"All we have to do is make it from here to the helicopter without getting shot," Mac said, "and we're off."

Kylie snorted. Running out in the open across an area void of vegetation would make them easy targets for getting shot in the back. However, they had no other choice. "I can't wait."

"Good, because we're going." Mac hustled her in front of him, using his body as a shield for any bullets that might fly at them from behind. They ran across the open field.

Mac forced them to zigzag to avoid being easy targets for whomever might be aiming in their direction. When she reached the helicopter, he gave her a boost up into the opening.

Josh scrambled aboard, Faaid came next and Tank set the Army Ranger on the floor of the chopper.

Mac's teammates converged on the helicopter.

"Are we all accounted for?" Mac asked.

"All except Dawg," Blade said. "Rucker's a little way back, covering for him."

Mac tilted his head and spoke into his mic. "Dawg, you on your way?" He waited a long moment, his brow dipping lower with each passing second. Then the frown lifted, and he nodded to the others. "He's on his way, and he's coming in hot."

The helicopter's blades thumped the air, as the pilot waited for the last man to load.

"Come on, Dawg," Kylie murmured for the Delta Force soldier she had yet to meet and thank for their daring rescue.

"Come on, Dawg," Mac echoed, his gaze on the village, his jaw tight. "Can't blow our record of no man left behind."

Kylie's breath caught and held in her throat.

She watched the shadows at the edge of town, praying for Mac's teammate.

Blade and Bull knelt twenty yards from the helicopter, their weapons trained on the village, waiting for Dawg to emerge from the shadows.

"Come on, Dawg," Mac muttered.

"I don't like it," Rucker said over the roar of the chopper rotors.

"Hold steady," Mac said. "He'll get himself out."

Bull rose from his position and started for the cluster of mud and stick homes.

At that moment, a silhouette appeared against the backdrop of the buildings and ran toward them, shifting right then left, hunkering low as he raced across the field.

"It's Dawg," Mac called out.

Dawg rushed for the helicopter.

Gunfire sounded from the village.

Blade and Bull returned fire from their positions.

When Dawg arrived at the helicopter, he leaped into the fuselage.

Bull and Blade backed toward the chopper, continuing to provide fire support until they, too, jumped inside. At that point, the gunner turned his machine gun on the village and let loose a stream of bullets.

The helicopter lifted up and away from the village, the rotors pounding the air, carrying them away. Hanging half out of the side of the chopper, the gunner continued to pour bullets down on Taliban gunmen.

Once they were out of range of the bullets, Kylie let go of the breath she'd been holding. "In case I didn't tell you," she shouted over the roar of the aircraft, "thanks for saving me."

He found her hand and squeezed it gently. "I'm glad I was there to do it."

The flight back took less than an hour. Bull worked on the Ranger to stabilize his wounds. Once they were on the ground at the base, medics appeared, transferred Sergeant Garcia onto a stretcher and loaded him into an ambulance.

"I don't suppose anyone can give Josh and me a ride back to my quarters in town?" Kylie asked.

Both Mac and Rucker shook their heads.

"We need you to come to our debrief, at least for the first few minutes," Mac said. "You'll have to let our CO know what you saw, heard and did. He'll need a clear understanding of the deaths of

Ahktar's brother and the other men. Then we'll have to decide what to do with you."

Kylie's brow furrowed. "What do you mean, what you're going to do with me? You're not responsible for me. I'm not a member of the military."

Mac's jaw tightened. "When an American citizen uses a U.S. military weapon to kill an Afghan citizen, that makes you my responsibility. If not my responsibility, then that of the American government. For now, you need to come with us." Mac caught her elbow and guided her away from the helicopter and toward the military buildings on the base. Rucker escorted Faaid and, along with Josh, followed with the rest of the team.

Kylie dragged behind. "I really need to get onto the video, edit it , add the story and get it to my boss."

"You're not going outside the wire until we say you're going outside the wire," Mac said. "And then, only when you have sufficient protection, so you don't get shot the second you step foot outside it." Mac's face softened. "Look, I know you're an independent woman, but right now, you're going to have a huge target on your back.

Please, go along with us and let us provide protection until we can hand you off to someone else."

Kylie's eyes narrowed. She chewed on her bottom lip. "You really think it's going to be that bad?"

"You're the investigative reporter. You've been in this war situation long enough...what do you think?" Mac asked.

Her lips pressed into a thin line. "Sadly, I think you're right. But that's really going to mess with my job here."

Mac gave her a twisted grin. "Then maybe you shouldn't have killed Mullah Ahktar's brother."

"It was them or me," Kylie said. "I chose him."

"I have no doubt you made the right decision," Mac said. "All I know is the Taliban will be embarrassed that a lowly female—no offense—took out three of their best soldiers, one of them being the brother of one of their leaders."

Kylie shook her head, her lips twisted. "I really didn't have time to ask him who he was when I shot him. He was trying to shoot me."

Mac and his team marched Kylie through the maze of temporary buildings and Conex box quarters and tents until they came to a metal structure. Rucker knocked on the door.

Someone inside called out, "Come in."

They gathered in what was a conference room or briefing center with the Delta team's commanding officer.

Rucker gave a brief explanation of what had occurred, and the role Kylie had played in killing Ahktar's brother.

The CO nodded his head when Rucker was finished and turned to Kylie.

"Sir," Kylie said. "I'm under contract to get my story out. Time is key."

The commander nodded. "And I'm under contract with the U.S. government to protect its people."

"I need to get to my hotel room and my computer," Kylie said.

The CO gave a chin lift to Dash and Rucker. "Send someone to this woman's hotel room and collect her belongings. She'll be staying on base until we can ship her out to Kabul."

A frown pinched Kylie's brow. "Don't I have a say in what happens to me?"

The commander shook his head. "You lost

that say when you chose to take a military weapon and shoot Afghan civilians."

"But they weren't civilians," Kylie protested. "They were members of the Taliban."

"But you *are* a civilian *and* a female," the commander said. "The Taliban won't like that you killed one of their own. Especially when they learn you're female."

Mac's lips twisted on the corners.

Kylie's eyes narrowed.

After the CO walked away, Kylie glared at Mac. "Don't you dare laugh."

He held up his hands in surrender. "I just know how you are. When someone tells you one thing and you want to do something else, you dig in your heels." His smile faded. "Look, Kylie, it's for your own good. You're going to have a price on your head."

The commander stopped at the door and turned back. "Mac."

Mac faced his commanding officer. "Yes, sir."

"I'm making you responsible for keeping an eye on our guest," the commander said.

"Thank you, sir…I mean, yes, sir!" Mac said.

The CO's brow furrowed. "Is that going to be a conflict of interest?"

"Sir?" Mac said.

"I take it that you two know each other."

Mac nodded. "Yes, sir. From way back."

"You know the rules about fraternizing in theater," the older man said.

"Yes, sir," Mac said.

"Don't let it happen," the commander said, with a stern look and left the building.

CHAPTER 3

Kylie nearly laughed at the way Mac stood so tall and straight while his commander told him not to screw up.

"It won't matter," Mac said. "Once burned, twice shy."

Kylie snorted. "I've never known you to be shy."

Mac's lips twisted. "Maybe not with people, but with old flames? Definitely shy." His lips thinned to a straight line as he stared into Kylie's eyes. "Guess you're stuck with me."

"What about me?" Josh the cameraman asked.

"If I'm staying on the base," Kylie said, lifting her chin, "my cameraman stays here, too."

"We'll arrange for quarters for both of you," Rucker said.

Kylie crossed her arms in front of her. "I really need to go back to my hotel room to bring back all the things I need—just so I have everything to make sure this story gets produced on time."

Mac glanced at Josh. "Do you know what she needs?"

Josh nodded. "I can figure it out."

Again, Kylie glared at Mac.

"Josh will go with the Delta team to retrieve the things you need from your hotel room and bring them back."

"Let's do it, then," Rucker said. "The sooner we get there, the less time we give Ahktar to figure out who your friend is and where she's been staying."

"She's not my friend," Mac said.

"Friend, girlfriend, whatever," Rucker said.

Mac's lips pressed together. "She's neither of those."

"Whatever," Rucker said impatiently. "She's your responsibility now."

"I guess you're right." Mac gave Kylie a frustrated grin. "While you guys are out, I'll make sure our guests are assigned adequate quarters."

Josh started for the door with the rest of the team to gather their things from the hotel room.

"I don't need a babysitter," Kylie groused.

Mac laughed. "Apparently, you do. And lucky me, I've been *volun-told* I'm it. Like it or not, you're stuck with me."

As Josh and the team left the conference room, Kylie called out, "You might want to leave your equipment with me."

"Oh, yeah." Josh handed her the camera.

Kylie didn't like that Josh was going without her. She felt a strong sense of love and responsibility for the cameraman who'd been with her on many dangerous shoots. "Be careful out there," Kylie said

"Who me?" Josh laughed. "I have an entire Delta Force team escorting me. I'll be all right. I'm more concerned about you. If I were you, I wouldn't walk too close to the fence. Don't make yourself any more of a target than you already are."

After the team left with Josh, Mac led Kylie to the logistics team to secure accommodations for her and Josh. He made certain that Kylie's quarters were in the empty unit beside his. "If you're not close, I can't protect you," he reasoned.

Once he'd secured their rooms, Mac showed Kylie where they were and let her ditch the camera inside. They stopped by the small hospital to check on Sergeant Garcia.

He'd already been stabilized and awaited transport via helicopter to the next level of care.

Kylie stood beside the sergeant's bed and touched his arm. "Thank you for saving my life and protecting me."

The sergeant smiled. "I should thank you for saving me."

She shook her head.

He took her hand and held it tightly. "It was my pleasure to protect such a pretty lady. It was worth the bullets."

"I don't know that it was worth the bullets. I didn't want anyone harmed on my account."

"All part of the oath," Sergeant Garcia said.

"What oath?" Kylie asked while squeezing the man's hand.

"The one to protect and serve."

"Well, thank you, sergeant. I hope you recover quickly."

"The doc said I should. I'll be back to my unit

soon. In the meantime, I get a free trip home. Haven't seen my wife and kids for six months. I'd say that was worth every bullet I took."

Kylie leaned down and kissed the soldier's cheek. "Tell your wife I appreciate your sacrifice. Thank you for your service."

"Glad I could help," he said with a sincere smile.

Then Mac showed her to the mess hall that operated 24/7 for people on all shifts. Mac chose a sandwich and a mug of steaming coffee. Kylie opted for a cup of hot tea and a piece of toast.

"You need to get more than that into your stomach," Mac said.

Kylie shook her head. "I'm not that hungry. I'm more concerned about Josh and your team getting back here safely. Think the Taliban will go after them?"

"It's possible. They were in that village, too."

Kylie's brow furrowed. "I should've gone myself."

"No, you shouldn't have. You're the one person they will want the most. If you'd gone, you'd have put the rest of them at risk."

"Good point," she said, nodding.

Mac ate half his sandwich before setting it

back on the plate and taking up his coffee mug. "Glad to see you got to where you wanted to go. Look at you, a war correspondent," he said and grinned.

Kylie sighed. "Hasn't been easy. People don't take women war correspondents seriously enough. I had to freelance it for a while."

"Are you still freelancing?" he asked.

"No," Kylie said. "I work for an international news syndicate. They fund my travel and lodging in exchange for gripping stories."

"I see you on all the news channels now," he said.

Kylie shrugged. "I don't know that I've *made* it, but I have moved up a little bit in this world. People don't look at me like I'm a crazy woman anymore." She smiled across the table at him. "And look at you. I remember you always wanted to be a part of the Delta Force."

He nodded. "I wouldn't have made it there without you."

Kyle frowned. "What do you mean?"

"If you hadn't dumped me when you did, I might not have gone for it."

She reached across and touched his hand. "I'm sorry."

"You had dreams. I had dreams. It just wasn't the right time for us."

She shrugged. "I couldn't have married you when I hadn't even begun living the life of my dreams. Speaking of married, what about you? Did you get married?"

He shook his head. "Being a member of Delta Force isn't conducive to long-term relationships. "So, the answer is no, I'm not married."

Kylie removed her hand from his.

"What about you? Did you tie the knot with some highly deserving man?"

"Being a war correspondent isn't conducive to long-term relationships. Most guys want a woman who will stay home and raise babies. I wasn't ready for that."

"Are you now?" Mac asked.

She shrugged, staring across the table at Mac, amazed that this man could still get her blood moving.

After she'd left him to get her career going, she'd had so many regrets. If there'd ever been a man who was right for her, that man was Mac. But they'd both been so young and ready to launch into their respective careers. He'd been on a path to get selected for Delta Force.

Kylie had been on the verge of pursuing her dream of becoming a journalist and a war correspondent. If they had continued their relationship and gotten married, she doubted seriously that either of them would've attained their dreams. He might not have become a Delta Force operative, and she might not have been in Afghanistan to interview an important informant from the Taliban.

Looking back over the years, and all the time they might have wasted, she wondered if she'd made the right decision in leaving him. Now that they were several years older and more experienced in both their fields, she was creeping up on thirty years old. As she'd neared her thirtieth birthday, she'd begun to feel her biological clock ticking.

Yes, she'd wanted a career, and she'd wanted it to happen before she had children. She'd known her line of work would be dangerous, and she wouldn't have left her child behind much less put that child at risk for losing a parent. So, she'd put her life on hold while she'd pursued her career.

Now, with her thirtieth birthday looming, she was concerned about being able to have children of her own. Some of her friends had waited until thirty to have kids. They'd found it difficult to conceive, as if they'd waited too long to try. Kylie had begun to think that she'd put her life on hold for all the wrong reasons.

And the only man who'd ever interested her was sitting across the table from her. Apparently, he still hadn't forgiven her for leaving him.

"What's next for you, Kylie?" he asked.

She'd been considering that for the past year. Did she want to remain a war correspondent, always chasing after the adrenaline and the next big story? Could she take a back seat and pick up human-interest stories that didn't put her in the line of fire, and actually start that family she'd put off for so long? Those thoughts went through her head as she tried to come up with an answer to his question.

Finally, she said, "For one, I want to interview Faaid."

He shook his head. "No, I mean what's the next thing you'll be doing in your life?"

She shrugged. "I don't know."

"How long do you plan on following war stories and putting yourself at risk?" he asked.

"It pays the bills," she said. "What about you,

Mac? How many years do you have in the military? Maybe fourteen? That gives you—what—six more years you can do this? What's next for you? Are you staying to retirement or longer? Are you looking ahead to see what you can do after retirement?"

His lips twisted. "Hadn't really thought much about it. Guess I was going to ride this horse into the sunset. Although, the older I get, the harder it is on my body. It's really a young man's world, being Delta Force."

She laughed, looking at his magnificent body. "You're far from old."

"Tell that to my knees." Mac grinned.

"Didn't you have a dream of having a ranch in Texas?" Kylie asked.

He nodded.

"Have you done anything about it?" she asked.

He stared into the distance. "I've been saving money, and I've got a real estate agent looking for a small patch of land I can call my own."

"So, you're going to be that rancher you always wanted to be and raise cattle and horses and children?" Her heart stuttered, as she waited for his answer.

"That's the plan," he said. "I'm not getting much younger."

"Have you met someone?" she asked before she could stop herself. "Don't answer that. It's none of my business."

He nodded. "As a matter of fact, I have."

Kylie's heart sank to the pit of her belly. She swallowed hard and said, "I'm happy for you. I hope she's special because you deserve someone special."

His lips quirked upward. "She is. And yes, I do deserve someone special."

She leaned across the table and touched his arm. "I'm sorry if I hurt you all those years ago."

His shoulders lifted and fell. "We were young. We got over it." Then he looked into her eyes. "So, have you met someone?"

She had. Many years ago. Kylie had never fallen out of love with him. Now, he sat across the table looking sexier and more mature than he had when they were younger. An intense ache settled across her chest. "Yes, I have met someone." She took a deep breath past the weight sitting on her lungs and changed the subject. "Do you think I can meet with Faaid, now?" She set her cup on the table, pushed back from the table and stood.

The thought of Mac with other women made her incredibly sad. The sooner she got her interview and left, the better.

"We can go and see if the intelligence guys are done with him." Mac rose from the table and stacked her tray on top of his. Once he returned the trays to the kitchen, he led her to the quarters he'd secured for her. By then, the team was back from the nearby town with Kylie's backpack.

Rucker handed her the backpack, and Kylie clutched it to her chest. "Thank you so much," she said, glad to have everything she'd brought with her to Afghanistan. "Did you have any troubles getting to it?"

Dash laughed. "Not really, because we're sneaky bastards. We saw a truckload of vicious-looking characters arrive at the front of the hotel. We went around the back, entered through the back door, and went straight up to your room."

"We guessed they'd have to ask which room you were in and that it would take time," Rucker said with a grin.

"We were in and out before the elevator made it up to your floor," Tank said. "We took the stairs down."

"How did you know they were Taliban or that they were coming to find me?" Kylie asked.

Dash puffed out his chest. "I stuck around in the stairwell long enough to see them break into your room. I left as soon as they did."

Kylie's eyes widened. "Wow. Thank you very much for getting my backpack."

Mac frowned. "All the more reason for you to stay on base tonight and to get the hell out of Afghanistan as soon as possible."

She sighed. "Fine. After I get my interview with Faaid."

"We'll arrange for that as soon as we get him out of Intel," Rucker said.

Dash tipped his head toward her quarters. "This is where you're staying?"

Kylie nodded. "Yes, it is. Why?"

Dash's lips split into a wide grin, and he jabbed Mac in the ribs with his elbow. "Lucky dog."

Mac frowned. "I had to put her in the room next to me because I have to keep an eye on her."

Dash nodded. "Uh-huh. You could've put her

next to any one of us, and we'd have gladly kept an eye on her."

"Knock it off," Mac said. "I'm the one the CO put in charge of keeping our guest safe."

If it had been any other man, Kylie would have accused Mac of being possessive, maybe even a little jealous. But surely by now, Mac was well over her. It had been years, and he'd just admitted he'd found another woman. Of course, she'd just admitted she'd found another man, too. None of the men she'd seen since Mac could compare to him. She'd never felt the same for them as she had for Mac. Yeah, she'd dated, but she'd always known they were only temporary. "Josh, where are you going to be?"

"Rucker set me up in a box around the corner from you. You want to work on that video I recorded during the mission?"

"The sooner we get it out the better," she said. He nodded.

She turned to Rucker. "How soon do you think it will be before I can see Faaid?"

"I'll check with the CO and see when we can get in to see him."

"In the meantime, I'll be here in my quarters, with Josh, working on what we have already."

For the next hour, Kylie and Josh edited the video. When they were happy with what they had, they agreed to take a break. It was late in the night, and Kylie was tired but still pumped up on adrenaline.

A knock sounded on the door. She opened it to find Mac standing there. "You can see Faaid now."

Her heart fluttered. "Josh, grab your camera, we're on."

Josh collected his gear and followed Kylie and Mac across the base to a building. Inside, Faaid sat with the commander.

"I got word from my chain of command that you're allowed to interview Faaid," the commander said. He stepped aside and waved toward the informant. "I'd like to sit in on the conversation, if possible."

"That will be fine," she said.

"Rucker's bringing the interpreter," Mac said.

A moment later, Rucker entered the building with another man in tow, an Afghan national who could speak English fluently.

Over the next hour, Kylie interviewed Faaid, using the interpreter, while Josh recorded the session and Kylie made notes.

When she had all the information she needed for her report, she thanked Faaid and wished him well. She hoped that he would be placed somewhere in the United States where he would be safe from the Taliban. With his cover blown, he wouldn't live long in Afghanistan.

Mac was waiting outside the door of the building to escort her and Josh back to their quarters. They dropped Josh off first, as his unit was closer. By the time they reached her room, it was the early morning hours. Still dark, people still asleep, the night shift working. She and Mac were alone, walking toward her quarters. When they arrived in front of her door, she reached for the doorknob and paused. "Thank you for saving my life and bringing me here to protect me."

"You're welcome." He turned her to face him and tipped her chin toward the starlight. "You look tired, Kylie."

"After a day like yesterday, it's to be expected. Anyone would be tired."

"No," he said. "You look tired, like you're tired of it."

She gave him a weak smile. "I'm living my dream. How could I be tired of it?"

"I'm living my dream, and I'm tired of it," Mac

said. "Delta Force is really a young man's work." He brushed a thumb across the corner of her mouth. "I used to love kissing you."

Her chest burned with longing. Not a day, not a week, not a year had gone by without her missing him. Right then she wanted to kiss him so badly, she started to lift up on her toes. Then she remembered that he'd said that he'd found another woman. She dropped down flat on her feet and stepped away. "That was a long time ago, Mac."

"Yes, it was. But if feels like yesterday." He bent until his lips hovered over hers. "I remember how you tasted."

His breath, warm against her skin, made her tingle. She swayed toward him as if drawn like a moth to a flame.

When their lips touched, a massive explosion rocked the earth next to them, knocking them to their knees.

CHAPTER 4

A SIREN REVVED UP, and the sound of heavy guns went off, lighting the sky with tracers.

Mac pushed her to the ground and covered her body with his. His teammates burst from the doors of their sleeping quarters, stepping out into the moonlight.

"What was that?" Kylie asked.

"C-RAM guns that detect and destroy incoming rockets," Mac explained.

Another explosion went off nearby and the Counter Rocket, Artillery and Mortar guns Kylie had heard of fired, making a burping sound, the rounds went off so fast.

Mac rolled off her, leaped to his feet, grabbed her hand and pulled her up. "Come on. We need to get to the bunker." With his arm around her, he ran her to the nearest reinforced bunker where they remained for the next thirty minutes.

After the initial attack, there were no other rockets launched at the forward operating base.

On their way back to their quarters, Rucker called out and ran to catch up to them. "The CO wants us in the conference room."

"I'm not leaving Kylie," Mac said.

Rucker nodded. "He wants her there, too."

Together, they hurried to the war room. Once inside, they found the CO and the rest of the team seated around the table.

"Just got word from Intel." The CO stared across the table at Mac and Kylie. "That attack was deliberate and meant as a warning message to our guest, Miss Adams. They'll leave this base alone, if we turn her over to the Taliban."

Mac stiffened beside Kylie. "No way in hell."

The commander lifted a hand. "We're not turning her over. However, we need to get her out of here. As long as she's here, she's a danger to all of the people on this base. As soon as we can arrange it, we're flying her out to Kabul. She'll catch the next plane back to the States."

"Sir, she won't be any safer in Kabul than she is here," Mac said.

The CO nodded. "And that's why you're going with her. Get some rest. Likely you'll be flying out at sunup, depending on the availability of helicopters."

"Yes, sir," Mac said.

"Miss Adams," the commander turned to Kylie, "stay safe."

"Thank you, sir," she said.

They returned to their quarters. This time when Mac stood outside her door, he took her into his arms. "You're in serious danger. Please tell me you're not considering staying in the country."

Kylie shook her head. "No, I've got my story. I'm done here."

Mac glanced down at her, his eyes narrowing. "You know, I don't think anyone can get onto the base, but if they do, they'll come looking for you in the unit they've assigned to you. It worries me that they might know where you are already."

"So," she said, "your concern is?"

He sighed. "Maybe we should switch quarters. You stay in mine; I'll stay in yours. That way if anyone tries to get into your room, I can take care of it immediately."

Kylie tilted her head to the side. "That makes sense, but that puts you at risk."

A gentle smile lifted the corner of his lips. "I'm more qualified to handle that risk."

"You have a point." Kylie ran her hand through her hair. "Okay. We'll switch quarters."

"Good," he said.

"This one's yours?" she asked, tilting her head to the room beside hers.

"Yes, it is," he said. "Let me grab a few things, and I'll take yours, you'll take mine."

"And I need to get my backpack," she said.

"Will you be going to the shower facility?" he asked.

She nodded. "I'd like to, after all the dust from the mission."

"Then we'll go at the same time," Mac said. "I'll stand outside while you shower. You can wait for me while I shower, as long as you don't go too far."

"Deal," she said with a grin. Kylie ducked into her room, grabbed her backpack and carried it over to his unit. Mac grabbed his toiletry kit and a change of clothes.

Kylie did the same.

Mac led her to the shower facility.

Inside, Kylie stripped down and stepped beneath the spray, soaping and rinsing quickly, then running shampoo and conditioner through her hair. It was a cold shower, but after the heat of the day, she just wanted to be clean and was thankful for the use of the facility.

She let the water run through her hair, rinsing the rest of the dust and conditioner out, remembering the times she'd shared the shower in her little apartment with Mac standing behind her, rubbing shampoo into her hair. He'd let the suds drip down over her body, and his hands would follow them over her shoulders, across her breasts and lower to the juncture of her thighs.

She was hot, even under the cool spray. Her desire for him hadn't waned in the least. In fact, if anything, it was even stronger.

By the time she toweled dry, she was wet in other places. She wished they weren't in Afghanistan but back in that little apartment. When she stepped out of the shower facility, she kept her head down and prayed he wouldn't see the signs of her desire in her eyes.

"Everything okay?" he asked.

"Yeah," she said briefly.

He touched her arm. "Are you sure?" His brow dipped. "You didn't get hurt in that explosion, did you?"

She shook her head. "No. I'm fine."

Where his hand touched her arm, it burned a path through her all the way to her core.

"While I'm getting my shower, wait here in the shadows. Scream if you feel threatened."

"I'll wait right here," she promised.

In less than five minutes, he was back out, smelling of soap, his hair dripping wet.

She chuckled. "You could have taken a minute to dry off."

He shook his head. "Nope. I was worried about you standing out here alone. I was afraid someone would take a shot at you."

"They'd have to take a shot from way past the fence line," she pointed out.

"Some of our guys have made shots longer than from here to the fence and hit their targets."

A shiver rippled down Kylie's spine as they made their way back to their sleeping quarters. "I'll keep that in mind."

Mac stood outside his own unit and waited

until Kylie stepped through the door. "There's a sleeping bag in the duffel bag. Just pull it out and spread it out on the cot." He touched her cheek with his hand. "When you close the door, make sure you lock it," he said and let his hand drop to his side.

Kylie said, "I will." With one last glance at Mac, she entered, shut the door and turned the lock.

The light was on, and she noted the space was barren, except for the duffel bag in the corner.

She crossed the short space to Mac's duffel bag, unbuckled it and pulled out the sleeping bag. As she did, a photograph slipped out. At some point in time, the picture had been laminated, but the edges were worn. She picked it up to put it back into the duffel bag.

When she turned it over, it wasn't a picture of the other woman he'd found, but of her and Mac all those years ago when they'd been young and in love. It had been taken at the state fair. They'd been riding on the Ferris wheel. At the top, they'd taken this picture of themselves. She'd been smiling up into his eyes when he'd snapped the shot.

Why would he carry a picture of them when

he had another woman? She laid the picture on the cot, and then spread out the sleeping bag. Still too warm to get between the folds of the sleeping bag, she lay on top of it, using it as a cushion against the tight canvas. The cot didn't have much give.

Knowing the morning would come soon, she lay down and closed her eyes. Then she remembered the photo between the bag and the cot. She fished it out and held it close to her heart.

He'd been hurt when she'd broken it off with him back then.

The fact he hadn't forgotten her made her heart swell. They had wanted different things back then. He'd wanted his Army career and for her to follow him, to be his wife and raise his children. She'd been in college, working on her journalism degree. He'd been about to ship out to Fort Bragg for his training in Special Forces.

When he'd asked her to marry him, she'd been two years short of finishing her degree. She hadn't been willing to abandon her studies and her dreams. Nor had she been ready to settle down and have children.

And he'd needed the time to dedicate to his training. It had to have taken a lot of skill and dedication to become Special Forces and then be selected for Delta Force.

Back then, she'd known he was the right person for her, but the timing had been wrong. Now that she'd been thinking about settling down and starting that family she'd always wanted later in life, it was too late to have him. He was still the right person for her, but he'd found someone else.

Kylie hugged the photo to her chest.

Was it too late?

With her eyes closed, she tried to sleep. When sleep didn't come, she let her memories flow back over all the time she's spent with Mac, the picnics they'd gone on, the hikes they'd made through Palo Duro Canyon, horseback riding at a local stable. They'd spent lazy days in the sunshine, floating the Guadalupe River.

Still shaken by the day's events and finding Mac again, Kylie lay wide awake. After thirty minutes of tossing and turning, she sat up, flung her legs over the side of the cot and stood. Crossing to the door, she listened for any sounds coming from outside.

Nothing.

She unlocked and tried to open the door, but

it wouldn't budge. Something was blocking the door.

Suddenly, it opened, and Mac stood there. "What's wrong?"

"Were you blocking my door?" Kylie asked.

He scrubbed a hand through his hair and gave her a weak smile. "I was sleeping there."

Her eyes narrowed. "You didn't go to bed?"

"No," he said and yawned.

"Why not?"

"I didn't feel comfortable leaving you alone," he said. "Besides, I can sleep sitting up."

She shook her head. "That's ridiculous."

"No, it's not. It's just not my preference on a long-term basis. Go back to sleep."

"I never went to sleep," she admitted.

His brow furrowed. "Are you worried there will be another rocket lobbed into this base?"

"I don't know. It's just that a lot happened. Between killing three Taliban terrorists, running into my old flame and being fired on with rockets, I'd say that's a pretty eventful day."

It might've been a mistake, considering Mac already had another woman he was interested in, but Kylie shook her head. "You might as well come in. We can sit up talking or staring at the wall until it's time to leave in the morning."

"Are you sure?" he asked, rubbing the back of his neck.

"I'm sure," she said.

He looked both ways. "I don't know. I might get busted for fraternizing in a war zone."

She snorted. "I'm not one of your military people. Surely it doesn't count."

His lips twisted into a wry grin. "I think any fraternizing counts, but I can keep a better eye on you if I can actually see you."

Kylie opened the door wider.

Mac stepped in, his broad shoulders filling the space. They were much broader than when she'd known him so long ago. Hell, he was as sexy, if not sexier than he'd been back then. Yeah, it might be a bad idea to bring him in, but she did it anyway.

MAC KNEW BETTER, but he went in anyway. He'd kissed her earlier, spinning up a whole slew of emotions he wasn't ready to deal with. Being alone with Kylie in confined quarters was a recipe for danger to his heart.

He squared his shoulders. All he had to do was keep his hands off her. She had someone else already.

Mac waited for Kylie to sit on the cot. Because there was nowhere else to sit, he sat beside her. That's when he spotted what she had in her hand.

"That's mine," he said.

She glanced at the photo with a smile. "Yeah, it fell out when I pulled your sleeping bag out of the duffel bag. Why do you still carry it?"

He shrugged. "It's been my good luck charm. It's gone with me on every deployment. I'm afraid if I leave it behind, something bad will happen."

She smiled. "Since when did you become superstitious?"

"As many missions and battles as I've been in, you tend to get that way. The one time I didn't bring it, I got shot in the arm." He raised the corner of his T-shirt to show her the scar.

"Maybe you were lucky you didn't bring it. Because if you had brought it, the bullet might've hit you in a much more lethal area," Kylie suggested.

"No, because every other time I brought it, I

never got shot." He tipped his chin toward the photograph. "Remember that day?"

She nodded. "I remember."

"Do you remember when the Ferris wheel got stuck at the top?" he asked. "That's when we took that picture."

She chuckled. "I remember we were up there for thirty minutes."

He smiled down at the picture. "We got quite a bit of necking in during that thirty minutes up there."

"Yes, we did," she said. "Those were good times."

"They were," he agreed. "And we were so young. I was barely out of bootcamp, and you were still in college."

"And look at us now," she said with a wistful smile.

"And look at us now," he said. "Sitting on a cot in Afghanistan, after being shot at by bullets and rockets." It felt good to sit close to her.

Kylie leaned her back against the metal wall and closed her eyes. "It's been a long day."

Mac pulled her over to lean against him. "Go to sleep. It will be too soon before we're heading out of here. You need some rest."

Kylie peeked through her eyelids. "You do too."

"I'll close my eyes," he said, "if you'll close yours."

"Deal." She yawned and kept her eyes closed. Soon, her breathing deepened.

For a long time, Mac sat with his arm around her, inhaling the scent of her hair. His heart squeezed tight in his chest. For so long, he'd dreamed of holding her again. Now she was with him...and yet...not. Mac had no right to be with Kylie. She had another man in her life. She'd given him up all those years ago. So, while he had the chance, he drank in every bit of her that he could. From the tips of her toes in her flip-flops, the well-defined muscles of her calves, her rounded kneecaps and the swell of her thighs, he absorbed her beauty.

At some point, he must have fallen asleep. The next thing he knew, there was a knock on the door.

"Mac," Rucker's muffled voice sounded outside his quarters. "Mac, are you in there?"

Mac slipped his arm from beneath Kylie, pushed off the cot and opened the door a crack. "I'm here."

"I knocked on Kylie's door," Rucker said, "but she didn't answer. Is she in there with you?"

"Yes, she is. It was the only way I could really keep an eye on her."

"That's good. We have a helicopter on standby. Can you two be ready in thirty minutes?"

Mac nodded. "We can."

"Grab some chow and meet us out on the helicopter pad."

"Roger," Mac replied, then closed the door and turned to Kylie.

She was off the cot, standing, rubbing the sleep from her eyes. "I'll be dressed and ready to go in less than thirty minutes."

"I'll wait outside," he said and headed for the door.

"Mac," her voice called out.

He paused with his hand on the doorknob, and then turned to face her.

"I missed you, too."

After stepping outside, Mac closed the door.

What did she mean by telling him *I missed you*? Did she still miss him? Did she want him back? What did she mean by that? Maybe she'd only missed him for a short time after leaving him. His head spun with the possibilities.

When Kylie finally stepped out, dressed in trousers, a long-sleeve blouse and a scarf wrapped around her head, he nodded toward her. "You might as well stay inside while I change. I want to keep an eye on you."

"Okay," she said. "I can turn my back. Although it's not like I haven't seen everything you've got." She winked.

His pulse ratcheted upward. He remembered seeing a lot more of her as well and was wishing he could again at that moment.

She reentered the room and stood to the side as he walked through the door.

While she stood with her back to him, he dressed in his desert camouflage uniform and boots. He strapped on his bulletproof vest. Although, the vest would do nothing toward protecting him from a broken heart. When he was done dressing, he gripped her arm, turned her and kissed her thoroughly. He set her at arm's length and said, "For old time's sake." Then he opened the door and, with a nudge, sent her through, stepping out beside her.

They walked across the base to the mess hall

and snagged a couple of fluffy biscuits and sausage patties to make breakfast sandwiches. They ate them quickly and hurried out to the helicopter pad where Rucker, Dash and Blade waited with Josh and Faaid.

"Where's Tank, Bull and Lance?" Mac asked.

"The CO didn't think we needed the entire team," Rucker said. "Just you to escort Miss Adams and her cameraman, and the three of us to escort Faaid. We're handing off Faaid to Intel in Kabul."

They climbed into the Blackhawk helicopter. Within minutes, they were off the ground and headed toward Kabul.

Mac sat beside Kylie, his thigh pressed against hers. That kiss had awakened so much inside him. He wanted more.

The flight was loud and not conducive to talk. He and Kylie sat in silence. He wished they were alone so he could ask her how she really felt about her new man, and to ask her if there was a chance they could rekindle that flame that had burned so brightly between them when they were younger.

Soon, they arrived at Bagram Airfield in

Kabul. Three vehicles were there to greet them upon arrival.

Rucker conversed with the drivers and came back to Mac and the others.

"We're keeping Faaid on base until he's transported out of the country. But we can't keep civilians here," Rucker said. "Miss Adams and Josh will be transported to a local hotel where me, Blade, Dash and Mac will provide security until you two are able to leave the country."

Blade and Dash escorted Faaid to the first vehicle. A security team of two climbed out, helped Faaid into the car and got in on either side of him.

Dash and Blade got into the second vehicle.

Mac and Rucker flanked Kylie in the back of the third vehicle. The driver slipped behind the steering wheel and drove them off the airfield and into the sprawling city of Kabul. He deposited them at the doorstep of a hotel from a major chain.

After being in the field around small villages built of mud and stick, it seemed incongruous to be standing in the opulent lobby of a five-star hotel in the same country.

At the desk, Mac asked for three rooms close together.

"Just three rooms?" Dash asked.

Mac nodded. "Rucker and Josh in one, Dash and Blade in another, and Miss Adams and I in the other. I'm not letting her out of my sight for a moment. After the rocket attack on the forward operation base, I wouldn't put it past them to attempt another attack here in Kabul."

"Good point," Dash said. "I'd gladly give you a break and take your spot," he said with a grin.

Kylie raised an eyebrow. "I think not. I know Mac. I don't know you, nor do I think I trust you."

Mac laughed out loud. "Good call. He's not known as Dash for nothing."

They got their room keys and headed up to the second floor on the back of the building. Mac inspected all three rooms and chose the one with a balcony overlooking a garden. Two of the rooms were side by side. The third was across the hall. Close enough that if he needed his teammates, all he had to do was call out.

As they stood outside their doors, Rucker asked, "So, what do we do with the rest of the day?"

"I don't know about you guys," Mac said, "but I'm going to catch some Zs."

"We didn't get much sleep last night," Dash agreed. "What do we want to do for dinner?"

"If any of you go anywhere, you should let us know," Mac said. "You could pick up some food and bring it back here."

"We can do that," Rucker said. "It wouldn't be a good idea for you two to venture out."

Mac nodded. "We had no plans to. Walking around the city would leave Kylie exposed to anyone who wanted to take a shot at her."

"Exactly." Rucker turned to Dash. "See you at 18:00, outside our doors. You and I can go out, get food and bring it back, so Mac and Miss Adams don't have to leave, and risk being shot."

"I like that idea," Mac said.

"So do I," Kylie agreed.

"18:00," Dash echoed.

Mac and Kylie entered one room. Rucker and Josh entered the one across the hall. Dash and Blade entered the room beside Mac's.

Once the doors closed, Kylie drew in a deep breath and let it out. "Too much drama," she said. "I don't know about you, but I could stand another shower after being up in that helicopter, stirring up dust."

"Agreed," Mac said, shrugging out of his bulletproof vest. "You can go first."

Kylie grabbed her backpack, carried it into the bathroom and left the door ajar.

Whether she meant to or not, that open door was too much temptation for Mac. He turned his back and walked to the balcony door, unzipping his jacket as he went. He sat in a chair, pulled off his boots and removed his socks. Every sound emitted from the bathroom made him look.

CHAPTER 5

MAC'S GROIN tightened as Kylie dropped her backpack on the floor, and stripped out of her shirt, shoes and pants. She stood in only her panties and bra, looking so incredibly sexy Mac couldn't catch his breath.

He reasoned that if she hadn't wanted him to see her, she would've closed the door. He marched toward her, stripping off his jacket, his blood pounding through his veins.

She stood with her back to him, her hands fiddling with the clasp on the back of her bra.

He entered the room, brushed her hands to the side and unhooked the garment. Then he pushed aside her hair and pressed his lips to the soft skin beneath her ear.

She leaned her head back against his chest and moaned. He slipped his hands over her shoulders, drawing the straps of her bra down her arms.

Kylie let the bra drop to the floor. Then she hooked her panties with her thumbs and shoved them over her hips and thighs. When they pooled at her ankles, she kicked them aside.

Mac's hands slid down her arms, down to her waist and followed the swell of her hips. He turned her to face him. His hands came up to cup her face between his palms, and he kissed her.

Her lips were every bit as soft as they'd been when they were much younger. She opened to him, her tongue meeting his in a dance he remembered so well.

She tugged his shirt from the waistband of his trousers and pushed it up his chest.

Mac took over from there, yanking it the rest of the way over his head and tossed it onto the counter. He made short work of his trousers and boxers, finally standing before her naked, his cock hard and jutting toward her.

He reached into the shower, switched on the water and waited, testing its warmth. Then he took her hand and led her into the stall, standing her beneath the spray.

Water ran over her head, onto her shoulders and dripped off the tips of her breasts. She was even more beautiful than she'd been the last time he'd stood naked with her when they were so young.

She ran her hands over his shoulders. "I don't remember you being quite this muscular," she said with a sexy smile.

"I think we've both changed."

Her eyebrows rose.

He amended, "For the better, of course."

She chuckled. "Matured."

"Matured is a good word," he said. "And you've matured beautifully." He tipped her head up and captured her wet mouth with his.

Her hands came up, laced around the back of his neck and pulled him down to her, deepening the kiss.

Mac squirted bodywash into his hand, lathered it up and smoothed it over her shoulders and collarbone. Working his way downward, he captured a nipple between his thumb and forefinger and pinched it gently.

Her back arched, pressing her closer to him.

She skimmed her calf along the side of his leg, wrapping it around the back of his thigh, pressing her sex against him.

He bent to take one of her nipples between his teeth, nipping lightly, tonguing it until it hardened into a tight little nub. When he'd tasted it thoroughly, he shifted to the other breast and treated it the same.

Meanwhile, his hands slid over her torso and down to the tuft of fluffy hair over the juncture of her thighs. He cupped her there, his finger dipping into her sex.

Kylie moaned, "Oh, my." She was so wet, and not just from the shower.

He stroked her there, dipping his finger in and out. Adding another finger, he swirled around inside then dragged his fingers up between her folds.

She drew in a deep breath and let it go against his chest. "I thought you found someone else."

His lips returned to hers, and he brushed them softly across her mouth. "I did. I lost her for a while, but fate brought her back to me." He leaned back and stared down into her eyes, his pulse racing, but the answers he sought were more important than quenching his physical needs. "What about you?"

"I lost him for a while but, like you said, fate brought him back to me," she said.

Mac's heart swelled. She still cared.

Kylie frowned. "I don't suppose you have protection, do you?"

He shook his head. "Sorry. I don't usually carry that when I'm deployed." His lips spread in a slow, sexy smile. "We don't need protection for what we can do."

"So true." She kissed him again and trailed her lips over his chin, across his chest and down his torso. The spray drummed over her shoulders as she knelt before him.

She circled her hand around his cock and ran it down to the base, fondling him there. Then she touched her tongue to the tip of his shaft.

Mac sucked in a sharp breath. His fingers laced through her wet hair. When she took him into her mouth, he groaned low in his chest.

Her hands moved around to cup his ass, guiding him into her, until the head of his dick touched the back of her throat. Then she pushed him back out, caressed the tip with her tongue and then took him inside again. Settling into a swift rhythm, she had him so hard and so tight, he couldn't hold back. He felt his release coming, jerked out of her and let loose. God it felt so good, his shaft pulsing and throbbing all the way to the end.

But he wasn't done with her. He soaked his palm with bodywash again and ran his hands over every inch of her body.

She returned the favor, touching him everywhere. Again, he grew hard and ready to take her, but he had no protection, and he wouldn't take her without it.

After they'd thoroughly rinsed, he turned off the water, grabbed a towel and dried her.

Kylie rubbed her towel over him, quickly soaking up the moisture.

When he could stand it no more, he swept her off her feet and carried her into the bedroom and laid her on the bed.

Mac leaned over her, claiming her lips. Then he trailed his mouth over her chin and down the long line of her neck, kissing, flicking and nibbling as he went. He stopped to graze on her breasts and then moved lower, slowly.

This was where he'd wanted to be all those years. Now, he was with her in Afghanistan of all places. Fate had played a huge part in bringing them back together. He couldn't screw it up this time.

KYLIE LAY against the sheets as Mac trailed his mouth across her body, tasting every inch until he reached the juncture of her thighs.

She widened her legs, giving him plenty of space to work his magic. He'd always been good about going down on her.

Inside, she was coiled so tightly it wouldn't take much to get her off. Mac had always been a considerate lover, making sure that he thoroughly satisfied her in every way.

He stroked her with a finger, dipping inside her, coming out covered in her juices. He swirled that wet finger along her clit.

She moaned and bunched the sheets in her fingers, raising her hips off the mattress, wanting more.

"You like that?" he said.

"You know I do," she said, her voice breathy, unable to draw in deeply when he was doing that to her.

"More?" he questioned.

"Please," she begged.

He swirled his finger around that nubbin of flesh, and then replaced his finger with his tongue, flicking it, knowing the exact pressure that set her off every time.

Her body tightened, her blood sizzled through her veins. Everything he did led up to one last important flick of his tongue that sent her flying over the edge.

Kylie gasped, grabbed his hair and held him there as he flicked, licked and strummed her like a musical instrument.

He didn't let up as she rode the wave of her orgasm to the very last throb. Kylie collapsed against the mattress, completely sated.

Mac chuckled, climbed up her body and lay down beside her, pulling her close.

She sighed. "How do you do that? You know the exact spot, the exact thing that makes me come apart every time."

He bent to nuzzle her earlobe. "Because I know you. Every inch of you."

Kylie nestled her head inside the crook of his shoulder, laying her cheek against his chest. She flung one of her legs over his and pressed her sex against his thigh, loving the way his hair was rough against her. God, it felt good to be close to him, skin to skin. She'd missed this so much.

He stroked her arm, her hip and the small of her back, pressing her closer to him.

Tired from being up all night, Kylie fell asleep, secure in his arms.

She slept hard and didn't wake until a couple hours later. When she opened her eyes, light still streamed through the window, but it was getting dim. It must have been getting close to the eighteen hundred meeting time the guys had agreed upon.

Kylie reached out for Mac but the space beside her was empty. She sat up and looked for him.

Mac stood with his back to the window, staring at her. "Yup, you're even more beautiful than you were when we were younger."

She lay naked against the sheets while he was fully dressed. "Hey, that's not fair."

He grinned. "What's not fair?"

"You're dressed. I'm not." She patted the bed beside her. "Come back to bed."

He shook his head. "No, I can't. It's getting close to six, and I promised the guys I'd meet up with them to talk about what to do for dinner."

She lowered her lashes and gave him a sexy smile. "You can send them out for food and come back for round two..."

He crossed to the bed, gathered her into his arms and captured her lips in a long, slow kiss that rocked her world. "I like the way you think."

"Do you think they could stop by a drug store and purchase some protection?" she asked.

He laughed. "No way. I'd never hear the end of it."

She pouted. "Such a shame." Leaning closer to his ear, she whispered, "I would've liked feeling you inside me. All the way inside me."

"Damn, woman, you're tempting." He smoothed a finger along the side of her cheek and down the length of her neck.

"Rucker looks like the responsible one," she said, her voice catching as his fingers brushed across one of her breasts. "Why don't you ask him?"

"I might just do that. In the meantime, you might want to get dressed. The guys will give me hell if I open the door and they see you lying in bed naked." He chuckled. "They already want to trade places with me."

She pulled the sheet up over her chest. "Not

interested in them," she said. "Now, you are an entirely different matter." With a wink she tossed back the sheet, swung her legs over the side of the bed and stood. "But if it makes you feel better, I'll get dressed."

"Trust me, it doesn't make me feel better. It makes me hard seeing you strut around the room wearing nothing but that sexy smile of yours." He caught her and pulled her body up against his fully clothed one.

Her skin tingled where the fabric of his T-shirt and trousers brushed against her. She hooked her leg around his and a hand behind the back of his neck. "You know, you don't have to go out at all. You could slip a note beneath the door or, better yet, call their room."

A knock sounded on the door.

He kissed her. "Too late. Grab your clothes and hustle into the bathroom, unless you want to give the guys an eyeful." A frown settled between his eyebrows. "That second suggestion is not really an option." He turned her around, swatted her ass and sent her toward the bathroom.

"Mac," Rucker's voice sounded through the door's paneling.

"Coming," Mac responded. "Go on," he said to Kylie.

She snatched her shirt, bra and trousers from the floor and ran for the bathroom, closing the door in time for Mac to open the outer one.

Kylie dressed quickly, her pulse pounding through her veins. She couldn't wait to see Mac again. She had a sudden, irrational fear that she would open the bathroom door and he wouldn't be there. Finding him, out of all the military personnel the U.S. had sent to the country, already seemed to be a minor miracle. Maybe she'd dreamed it all.

After she was fully dressed, she ran a brush through her hair in an attempt to tame the wild tangles left over from going to sleep with damp hair. Giving up, she pulled her hair back in a loose ponytail at the nape of her neck.

With a quick glance at her reflection, she sucked in a deep breath and opened the bathroom door.

The room was empty.

Her breath caught and held in her throat as she raced across the room to the door leading into the hallway. Without slowing to press her eye to the peephole, she yanked open the door and ran into Mac's back.

"Oh," he said and turned. "There you are. Blade, Josh and Rucker are heading out in search of food. Anything in particular you might like to eat?"

She shook her head. "Josh knows what I like. I'll trust your selections," she said to Rucker. "As long as it's not raw."

"That leaves our choices wide open." Rucker glanced from Kylie to Mac and shook his head. "You probably don't care as long as we get out there and get back."

"You got that right," Mac said. "In the meantime, we'll remain holed up in our room until you return."

"It's a tough job..." Dash started.

"But someone has to do it," Mac finished.

Dash snorted. "Yeah, yeah. I'll stick around and provide backup for you guys. I thought I'd stake out the lobby and circle the building to look for any potential dangers. I'll have on my earbud headset." He touched a finger to his ear. "Mac, you might want to keep yours on. If anything happens, I'll be able to relay information to you quickly."

Mac nodded. "I'll put it on as soon as we go back into our room."

"We'll have ours on as well," Rucker said. "If we see anything, we'll relay the information to you. Any questions?"

They all shook their heads.

"Take care of yourselves and remain alert," Rucker said. "Ahktar's men play for keeps."

Mac led Kylie back into their room and closed the door. He crossed to his bulletproof vest and fished in one of the pockets for a small headset and pressed it into his ear.

"Comm check," he said and waited. "I read you loud and clear. Hurry back. Getting hungry here." He glanced across at her. "What do you want to do while we're waiting for our food to arrive?"

Kylie rubbed her arms. "I don't know." She tilted her head toward the television. "We could see if there's a news channel."

"It could be fun guessing what they're saying," he said. "Or we can sit and talk."

She glanced toward the bedroom. "I'd suggest going back to bed, but…"

His lips twisted. "Without Rucker and Blade as backup, it might not be a good idea."

"We could make out?" she suggested, batting her eyelashes.

He growled and stalked toward her. "Excellent idea." Scooping her up, he carried her to the couch, sat with her in his lap and nuzzled her ear. "I've missed this."

"Me, too." She leaned her head back to give him better access to her neck.

She hoped the guys would take a little longer finding their food. Making out with Mac was more important. Who knew when they might run into each other again?

CHAPTER 6

MAC TASTED KYLIE'S skin from her earlobe to the base of her throat where her pulse beat strong and fast. He couldn't get enough of her.

All too soon, she'd leave on the next plane out of Afghanistan. Then what?

His arms tightened around her. He didn't want to let go. Not now...not ever.

"What next, Kylie?" he murmured against her skin.

"My breast," she answered, her voice breathy as if she couldn't get enough air in her lungs.

He chuckled and raised his head. "No, I mean what's next for us?"

She sighed and leaned her forehead against his. "I don't know. You tell me."

"I know how important your career is to you," he said. "I would never want you to give it up for me."

"And I know how much you love being a part of the team." She took his face between her palms and pressed a kiss to his lips. "Where does that leave us?"

"Between a rock and a hard place," he said with a grin, shifting his hips so that she could feel how hard she made him. "But really. Do our careers leave any room for a relationship?"

"I guess it depends on what you consider a relationship?" she said. "If you want a woman who stays home and bakes cookies for all your teammates, I'm not your gal."

He laughed out loud. "I remember how you baked cookies. You forgot them in the oven, set off smoke alarms and had the fire department out to douse the fire."

She frowned. "I've gotten better. I only burn one of four trays of cookies now. I call that progress."

He kissed her lightly. "I don't need a chef to bake my cookies. I need someone to love whenever we can get together. I haven't found too many women who can deal with an absentee husband and father. Delta Force soldiers are on call and can be deployed at a moment's notice. I can't ask anyone to put up with that kind of uncertainty. It's hard on a marriage. I've seen too many Deltas divorce after less than a year of marriage."

"Those women didn't understand what they were signing up for."

"And you do?" he asked.

She shrugged. "I have a clue. My career has been much the same. Once I got the gig of war correspondent, I've been on call 24/7. I could fly out at a moment's notice. Not too many men can deal with a wife who's never at home to greet him after a hard day at the office."

"So, we're back to the question of where does that leave us?" Mac said.

"I think if two people care enough about each other, they can make anything work," she said softly.

"Does that mean you care?" he asked, his chest tight, his hands gripping her arms.

Kylie opened her mouth, but before she could say anything, the earbud in Mac's ear crackled.

"Mac," Rucker's voice blasted into his head,

jerking him out of a possible future, back to the present.

He pressed a finger against the communications device. "I read you."

"Got trouble coming," he said, his breath huffing across the airwaves as if he were running. "We're on our way back."

"What trouble?" Mac asked, scooting Kylie off his lap onto the couch beside him. Then he pushed to his feet.

"Truck load of men in black outfits and turbans. Can't be sure, but they might be Ahktar's—"

"They're here at the hotel," Dash's voice interrupted. "I'm heading up the stairwell. Mac, get Kylie out of the room and on her way out of the building."

"On it," Mac said.

"What's going on?" Kylie whispered.

Mac grabbed her hand and started for the door. "Time to bug out."

"Damn, they don't give up, do they?" she said as she snagged her backpack on the way through the room.

Mac pushed through the door. "Apparently, Ahktar gave a damn about his brother."

"Or his pride," Kylie said, lowering her voice as she stepped out into the hallway behind Mac.

The stairwell door at the end of the hallway burst open.

Mac ducked down, taking Kylie with him.

When he saw Dash running toward them, he straightened.

"Can't go back that way," Dash said. "It leads to the hotel lobby and more than half a dozen Taliban terrorists." He kept moving, passing them in the hallway, racing past the elevator toward the other end of the building. "Come on," he called out. "This way leads out the back."

Mac moved Kylie in front of him. "Run," he urged.

Kylie took off, catching up to Dash as he opened the door to the other stairwell.

Mac was right behind her and heard the elevator ding as he rushed through the door.

He dared to look back through the window to see four men in black garb and turbans rush from the elevator car into the hallway, turning toward the room where he and Kylie had been moments before.

"They're in the hallway," Mac announced in a

muted tone. He spun to find Dash climbing the stairs instead of going down.

"Trust me," Dash called out softly, leaning over the rail above. "You have to go up before you can go down."

Kylie was already halfway up the stairs, moving quickly and quietly.

Mac ran after her. They had to get out of the stairwell before the Taliban men discovered they'd missed them and went looking.

Dash led them up a flight, down a long hallway, around a corner and into another stairwell that led downward. When they reached the bottom, the door opened into a huge laundry room filled with commercial-grade washers and dryers as well as giant machines for ironing the sheets. A couple men dressed in white staff uniforms worked folding sheets, tablecloths and towels.

As Mac ducked through, he heard shouts behind him in the stairwell. He let the door close quietly and hurried to catch up with the others. As he reached Kylie and Dash, he called out over the roar of the machines, "We have company headed this way."

Dash nodded and pushed open a door on the

other end of the laundry room. He rushed through, Kylie on his heels.

Mac followed, worried they weren't moving fast enough. What if they got out of the building only to find the Taliban had set up a perimeter around the structure to keep them from escaping unnoticed?

Dash was one of the best Deltas Mac knew. He would check before running out into the open.

They moved down another hallway, off which were the kitchen and a storage room. For a split second, Mac considered hiding out in the storage room among boxes of supplies. He immediately squelched that thought, not liking the idea of being a sitting duck, waiting for the Taliban to find them.

The door at the end of the hallway opened onto a loading dock where men worked moving crates and boxes from trucks to stack them on the concrete.

One of the men shouted at them and waved his fist.

Dash kept moving down a set of concrete stairs and out into an alleyway behind the hotel.

A large block wall separated the hotel grounds from the other buildings nearby.

With little time to spare and a long wall to follow if they wanted to go around it, Dash shook his head, cupped his hands and said, "You first, Mac."

Mac ran toward him, placed his foot in his friend's hands and leaped up to the top of the wall, pulling himself up to straddle the top. Then he leaned over and reached for Kylie's hand.

She stepped into Dash's cupped hands, grabbed Mac's outstretched one and let him pull her up onto the wall.

A shout from a window above made Mac look up.

A man dressed in black stood on a balcony shouting down at them. He raised his rifle to his shoulder and shot down at them.

Mac shoved Kylie over to the other side, holding onto her hand. She dropped, her grip on him slowing her fall until she landed lightly on her feet.

Mac reached down, grabbed Dash's hand and swung him up to the top.

As soon as Dash had his leg over the top, Mac

let go. His teammate let his momentum carry him over the top and down the other side.

Another shot rang out. Something stung Mac's shoulder. He grunted and tipped over, dropping to the ground. Pain throbbed in his left arm. He winced but kept moving.

"You're hurt," Kylie said, running with him alongside the wall.

"I've been hurt worse," he said through gritted teeth. "We have to get out of here. That man will alert his buddies, and we'll have all of them after us soon."

Mac led the way this time, keeping Kylie close beside him.

"We're almost back to the hotel," Rucker said into his headset.

"We're out of the hotel, moving away from the back into the city," Mac said.

"Good," Rucker said. "We're coming up from the rear."

As Mac emerged from an alley into a busy road full of cars, bicycles and people walking, he realized they were in a marketplace.

"I see you now," Rucker said. "We're by the rug dealer, twenty yards to your left."

Mac searched the crowd and found Rucker,

Josh and Blade hurrying toward them. When they screeched to a stop, Mac shot a glance over his shoulder. His heart skipped several beats, and his blood ran cold.

Five men in black garb ran through the marketplace, pushing and shoving people out of the way. They brandished AK-47s and shouted something that made the crowd of people duck down.

"Get down," he yelled and forced Kylie into a hunkered position as they ran.

Dash leaned over and raced to a gap between buildings. "This way," he shouted.

Rucker and Blade joined them and knelt at the corner of buildings to provide cover when the Taliban got closer.

Mac had his Glock pistol tucked beneath his jacket, but he couldn't shoot it in a crowded marketplace full of civilians that included women and children.

That didn't stop the Taliban.

They fired their rifles at the Deltas.

Women screamed and fell to the ground, covering their children with their bodies.

Urging Josh to lie flat against the ground, Rucker and Blade stayed low but didn't shoot back. With their only weapons the pistols they'd worn inside their jackets, they had to wait for the terrorists to move dangerously closer before they returned fire.

Mac shoved Kylie between the buildings, but they were far from out of the woods. The men with the guns would follow, hunting them down until they killed them.

Unless the Deltas killed Ahktar's men first.

That meant getting them out of the market into a less crowded area where they wouldn't incur as much collateral damage.

Mac prayed they had enough time to get to a defensive position and set a trap. He refused to let this be the way his and Kylie's relationship ended. He wanted more.

CHAPTER 7

Kylie ran, determined to stay abreast of Dash and Mac as they did their best to keep her alive. She hated the thought of one of them dying because of her. They'd done so much to keep her safe. The least she could do was keep up.

Her lungs burned, and her breath came in short gasps as she ran and ran, following Dash, and then Mac and now Dash, again, through the maze of Kabul's city streets.

She glanced back at every turn. Rucker and Blade were close behind them, ready to defend them as they ran.

As they moved from the business district to the residential area, the buildings became denser, but there were fewer people on the streets.

"We can't keep running," Mac said as they entered a narrow street with single-story homes on either side. "This will do to set up defense."

"Give me a boost," Dash said.

Mac cupped his hands.

Dash stepped in and swung up over the wall surrounding a home, disappearing onto the other side.

Rucker, Josh and Blade caught up.

"They're a block behind us, heading this way," Rucker said. "We don't have much time."

"Dash, is it clear?" Mac called out.

"Clear," Dash responded. "We have a woman and two small children."

"Come on, Kylie. Over the wall." He lifted her in his arms.

She wrapped her arms around his neck. "I'd rather stay with you."

"I need to focus on taking these men down. If I'm worried about you, I could put myself and my team at risk."

She nodded. "Okay. But I don't like it. If you have another gun, I could help."

He kissed her and swung her to the top of the wall. "For now, your shooting days are over. Keep your head down. These walls may or may not stop bullets." He spoke into his headset. "Kylie's coming over."

Kylie slipped down the wall on the other side. "Hey, what about Josh?"

"They're not after Josh. But we'll keep him safe," Rucker responded.

Dash stepped to the door of the home and waved Kylie inside.

A woman cowered in the corner of the front room, clutching her children to her breast.

"We're not here to hurt you," Kylie said.

"They don't speak English," Dash said. "Stay here and stay down." He left her and ran back outside. A moment later, she heard footsteps on the roof.

Kylie glanced at the woman and children, feeling awful about invading their home. They appeared terrified. One of the small children sobbed quietly.

His mother held him close, whispering softly, urgently. The child hiccoughed and sniffled.

Outside in the street, shouts sounded, and gunfire erupted.

Kylie sat on a carpet and kept her head down, praying the Deltas were successful and stopped the Taliban terrorists. She wouldn't be safe until they did. And they wouldn't be safe if they continued to protect her.

As she hunkered close to the floor, she stared across the room at the woman and her children. She hated that they were afraid of her when she meant them no harm.

Fumbling in her pocket, she pulled out a package of Lifesaver candies she liked to suck on when she was nervous. She hadn't opened them yet, determined to have some left for the trip back to the States.

While the gunfire continued outside, she eased her way across the floor, stopping five feet from the woman and her children. Then she held out her hand with the roll of candies.

The children shrank against their mother.

Realizing they were too afraid to come get the candy, Kylie set the package on the floor and gave it a gentle push, sending it rolling toward the kids.

She backed away, letting them know she wasn't a threat.

For a long moment, the children clung to their mother, the gunfire still going off outside the walls of the home.

Kylie felt sorry for the family. They were

probably used to those sounds, having heard them all too often.

After a minute or two, the oldest child leaned away from his mother and reached for the candy on the floor. Once he had it in his hand, his mother yanked him back to her side.

The two children hovered over the package of hard candy. The mom kept her eye on Kylie.

Kylie smiled at the woman. "It's okay. I won't hurt you," she said softly.

The gunfire slowed and finally seemed to stop.

Had the Deltas taken down all the men who'd been following them?

When they didn't come right in to get her out, she worried that maybe the Taliban men had taken out the Deltas.

She shook her head. That wasn't possible. The Deltas were highly trained. They couldn't be defeated by five or six Taliban terrorists.

The woman sitting on the floor across from her stiffened, her eyes growing wide. She made a small sound that caught Kylie's attention, and her gaze darted to something over Kylie's shoulder.

Kylie spun too late to deflect the blow to her head that sent her flying across the room. She lay for a moment. Her head spun, and her vision blurred. She thought for a moment she'd pass out.

Someone grabbed her arm, yanked her to her feet and shoved a pistol against her temple. He shouted something in a language she couldn't understand, even if she wasn't about to black out.

Then he was shoving her toward the door, his free arm clamped around her middle, trapping her arms to her sides.

"Let me go!" she said, her voice slurring, her vision fading from clear to black and back to clear. She stumbled, almost taking him down with her.

He yelled again.

The children on the other side of the room sobbed. Their mother clutched them to her, turning away to place her body between them and the gunman.

A fleeting thought raced through her muzzy head. If she could only remember the Krav Maga techniques she'd learned, she could take this bastard down.

But she could barely stand, much less fight.

When he reached the door, he lowered the gun long enough to pull the door open. Once it was wide enough, he pushed her in front of him, yelling. "I kill! I kill!"

The longer she stood, the clearer her head got. She had to pick the right time to kick the man's ass, or he'd pull the trigger and blow her brains out before she could twitch a finger.

Where was Mac? They weren't shooting anymore. Were they all dead? Was this guy one of the Taliban terrorists?

Dash dropped from the roof to the ground in front of the man, raising his hands. "Don't hurt her," he said, "and we won't hurt you."

The man holding her banged the barrel of his pistol against her temple, sending a sharp stab of pain through her head.

Anger pushed aside the fuzzy gray shroud of dizziness.

Taking a deep breath, she went limp, dropping down through the man's arms. His grip slipped, and the gun in his hand rose above her head.

Then she came up fast and hard, tipping her head back, catching his chin with her skull.

He jerked backward and lost his hold on her.

Kylie dove forward.

The man behind her was slammed sideways,

hitting the ground with a thud with Mac on top of him.

The Delta Force soldier pinned the man's wrist to the ground, banging it until he released the gun.

Dash kicked it out of reach, and then picked it up.

Once he'd lost his weapon, the man cried out. "No kill, please. No kill."

"Why should I spare you when you tried to kill my woman?" Mac growled.

"No kill."

"Mac," Kylie called out. "Don't kill him. I think that's his wife and children inside."

"He threatened to kill you," Mac said, his face ferocious.

"I'm okay." Kylie laid her hand on Mac's back. "He didn't kill me. Let him up."

Mac remained on top of the man for another long moment then climbed to his feet. He yanked the man up and twisted his arm behind his back.

The woman and small children burst from the home and ran toward the man.

The little boys wrapped their arms around his legs and cried. The woman stood in front of the man, talking fast to Mac, her hands clasped together as if begging him to let her husband live.

"He was just protecting his family," Kylie said.

"He almost killed you," Mac said, his voice low and rough.

"But he didn't," Kylie repeated. "You can let him go. I don't think he'll hurt us."

"Go ahead, Mac. I've got you covered." Dash held his weapon trained on the father.

Mac released the man. He turned and pushed his wife and children behind him. Then he bowed, pressing his hands together. "Thank you. Thank you."

Mac pulled Kylie into his arms. "I died a thousand deaths watching him press that gun to your head."

"Wouldn't have done him much good," Dash said. He held the gun in his hand, the bolt open and empty. "It wasn't loaded."

Kylie laughed. "Now, I feel bad for hitting him with my head."

"I don't feel bad." Mac brushed his thumb lightly across her temple. "He hit you."

"I'll live," she said. "Those kids have been through enough. I'm sure this isn't the first time they've been scared."

Rucker entered through the gate of the walled home. "We've checked. The threat has been neutralized."

"We can't go back to the hotel," Mac said.

"I've contacted the air transport folks at Bagram Airfield," Rucker said. "They have a plane they can get Miss Adams on tonight. We just have to get her there in the next hour to fill out the paperwork."

Dash glanced at this watch. "That doesn't give us much time. I doubt we'll find a taxi this far away from the city center."

Kylie stared up into Mac's eyes. "I'm flying out tonight."

His gaze never left hers. "You are." He gripped her arms and pulled her close, resting his chin on her hair.

Dash tapped his watch. "What part of *we don't have much time* do you not understand?"

Blade elbowed him. "Shh, man. Can't you see they're having a moment?"

Rucker chuckled. "We can wait for a moment, but much longer than that, and she might miss that flight."

"Would that be a bad thing?" Mac murmured.

She nodded. "It keeps you all at risk. I have to

go." Kylie's heart was breaking, but she stepped back. "We need to get moving."

"Are you up to walking really fast?" Rucker asked. "That blow to the head had to have hurt."

She nodded, wincing. "It did. But I'll be okay." Avoiding Mac's gaze, she glanced around. "Any idea how to get back to a place where we can catch a taxi?"

The man who'd hit her looked up. "Taxi?"

Kylie nodded. "Yes. Taxi."

He waved his hand toward the gate. "Come. Taxi."

He led, and the Deltas followed, their weapons at the ready.

Mac stayed at Kylie's side, hovering over her, using his body as a shield.

With each step, Kylie fought back tears. In a few short hours, she'd be on her way back to the States. She didn't know when she'd see Mac again, or if he wanted to see her. They'd been together, made love and had fallen right back into the easy way they'd been with each other so long ago. But was that enough? Or had this just been a fling on his part? A way to get her out of his system?

The Afghan led them to another walled home

and through the gate. Inside the yard was a small van with a sign on top.

"Taxi." He nodded and then went to the door, banging loudly.

An older Afghan answered. The two spoke, and the older man went back inside and came out with a set of keys.

"Where do you want to go?" the older man asked as he walked toward the vehicle.

"Bagram Airfield," Rucker responded.

The six of them crowded into the van, and the old man slipped into the driver's seat. Soon, they were on their way through the city toward Bagram Airfield and the plane that would take Kylie away from Mac.

Kylie sat between Dash and Mac, holding Mac's hand. He squeezed tightly, the pressure bringing tears to her eyes. Not because it hurt, but because it might be the last time they held hands for a long time.

She didn't want to let go.

MAC LIKED the feel of Kylie's hand in his. For years he' dreamed of holding her, of loving her and making her his.

With her back in his life again, he didn't want to let go.

The taxi slowed at an intersection, and the driver waited for traffic to pass before he could merge.

A vehicle slowed and allowed them to join the long line heading in the direction of the airfield.

Two blocks later, the van came to a complete stop.

"What's holding us up?" Mac leaned forward, looking over the driver's shoulder.

Rucker, in the front passenger seat frowned. "I don't know, but I'm going to find out." He glanced over his shoulder as he pushed open his door. "Comm on?"

"Roger," Mac said.

The others responded in kind.

Rucker dropped down from the van and walked at a determined clip alongside the standing vehicles, disappearing within seconds.

Mac held his breath, a bad feeling making his gut knot. Thankfully, he was on the side of the van with the sliding door. If something threatened them, he'd be out on the street with Kylie in less than a heartbeat.

"Damn," Rucker said into Mac's ear.

"What?" Mac shot back, his gut screaming for him to reach for the doorhandle.

"Got a checkpoint up here…manned by our trusty men in black. On my way back. Get the hell out of the van and go."

Before Rucker completed his sentence, Mac had the sliding door open and he was out on the pavement, dragging Kylie out with him.

"What?" she asked, her gaze shooting the direction Rucker had gone.

The other members of his team climbed out behind them.

Mac, holding onto Kylie's hand, turned back the direction from which they'd come and walked fast, putting as much distance as possible between them and the checkpoint.

"They spotted me," Rucker said. "Run!"

Mac's hand tightened on Kylie's as he took off, pushing past pedestrians and cyclists, attempting to get around the parking lot of vehicles in the street.

As if they were swimming upstream, Mac waded through the throngs of humanity, trying to get Kylie to someplace safer.

Ahead, he heard the sound of shouts and a woman's scream.

The crowd of people on the sidewalk parted.

Half a dozen men in the black uniform worn by Ahktar's Taliban soldiers appeared, shoving people out of the way, waving their AK-47s and shooting as they stormed through the crowd.

"Got more trouble from the other end of this wagon train," Mac reported. "Heading east off the main drag."

"We've got your back," Dash said. He and Blade stopped at the corners of the buildings flanking the road Mac turned onto.

He leaned down to speak into Kylie's ear. "We need to move out sharply. You up to it?"

She laughed. "Do I have a choice?" Picking up the pace, she broke into a sprint.

Mac had to hurry to keep up with her.

They ran a long block and cut back north.

"Keep going," Dash urged. "We're behind you, trying to stay out of sight of our friends.'

"Sorry, guys," Rucker's voice cut into Dash's report. "I've been spotted. I'll try to lead them away. Problem is, now they know we're out here."

Mac's grip tightened on Kylie's hand.

"I'm going with Rucker," Dash said into the radio. "Someone has to cover his ass."

"What am I missing?" Kylie asked, looking up at Mac's face as they moved through the streets.

"Rucker was spotted. The Taliban now knows we're close," Mac said. "Dash is dropping back to cover for Rucker. It's you, me, Josh and Blade." He glanced back as Blade brought up the rear of their small group.

Blade said something to Josh. The two moved faster to catch up to Mac and Kylie.

"Shit, Mac," Blade huffed. "We've got a tail of four guys in black."

"Gotta move faster," Mac said.

Kylie was breathing hard. She'd started to slow her pace, but he gripped her elbow and helped her to go faster.

He dared to look back at the men trailing Blade and Josh. They were raising their rifles to their shoulders. If Mac didn't get Kylie out of the line of fire, she might be hit.

He rounded the next corner at a sprint and came to a skidding halt.

A dozen men were dropping down from a truck, each carrying a rifle.

A shout went up, and they rushed toward Mac and Kylie.

Josh and Blade raced around the corner,

running into Mac and Kylie, sending them lurching forward.

The Taliban encircled them before Mac could do anything to stop them or get away.

"We've been surrounded," Mac whispered into his mic, holding up his hands as a dozen rifles pointed at Kylie, Mac, Josh and Blade. "We have no choice. Surrender or die."

"Calling in the rest of the team," Rucker said. "We'll find you. Just do us a favor and stay alive until we do."

"Roger," Mac said without moving his lips.

At that moment, one of the men in black grabbed the radio earbud from Mac's ear, threw it on the ground and stomped on the device. He jerked his head toward the others. The men searched Kylie, Josh and Blade, finding the earbud in Blade's ear and destroying it in the same manner.

They frisked the four of them, removing guns, knives and ammunition from Mac and Blade. The Deltas were forced to remove their bulletproof vests, and then they were searched again.

When the Taliban soldiers were satisfied, they tied their wrists behind their back with zip-ties, slipped black hoods over their heads and shoved them into a van that had pulled up behind the truck the men had arrived in.

Mac hated that he'd failed to protect Kylie. He should have gotten her away from the traffic jam sooner. He should have put up a fight with the men who'd captured them.

No. He'd done the only thing he could. If he'd tried to fight the dozen or so men, he might have picked off three or four, but not all twelve. They'd have shot him dead. Once the bullets started flying, they wouldn't stop until Mac, Blade, Josh and Kylie were dead on the ground.

Being captured alive gave them a second chance to come out of the situation alive. Mac would do everything in his power to make that happen.

CHAPTER 8

WHEN THEY'D FLUNG Kylie into the van, she'd hit her head on the floor. The force of the blow made her black out. It wasn't until she heard the sound of Mac's voice whispering to her that she came to.

"Kylie," he said so softly, she wasn't certain if she was hearing him or dreaming that they were alone together in the darkness of the hotel room, about to make love again.

A jolt woke her the rest of the way, reminding her she was lying on cool, hard metal, not a soft mattress. And the darkness had nothing to do with night, but the bag they'd draped over her head.

"Mac?" she responded softly.

"Are you okay?"

"I think so," she said, moving her legs. She tried to move her arms, but a hard strand of plastic around her wrists kept them motionless.

"Josh?" she whispered.

"I'm okay," he responded from somewhere behind her.

"Blade?" she asked.

"Here," he said.

A voice shouted in Pashto, and someone popped Kylie in the side of the head.

She grunted and lay still.

"Bastard," Mac said and moved beside her, as if trying to rise up.

The crack of plastic on something hard sounded, and Mac dropped to the hard floor of the van and lay still.

Kylie's heart leaped into her throat. "Mac?"

Again, a man shouted in Pashto. Expecting to be slapped again, Kylie hunkered down. Instead of a hand, something hard and plastic slammed into her head.

Pain shot through her temple, and she blacked out.

How long she was unconscious, Kylie didn't know. A rush of cool air revived her, and she realized the van was no longer moving.

Hands reached out to grab her arm. She was dragged from the van by two men, one on either side. They barely let her get her feet beneath her before they marched her across uneven ground.

The creak of door hinges sounded. The two men on either side of her shoved her hard, sending her flying forward. She landed on her knees on a dirt floor, the forward momentum taking her the rest of the way down. With her hands tied behind her back, she had no way to slow her fall. Kylie landed on her face, the jolt making her head swim from the pain.

The creaking of hinges sounded again, and then silence reigned.

"Mac?" she called out, her voice the only thing she could hear. "Mac?" Panic rose up her throat, threatening to choke her. "Josh, Blade?"

She couldn't see, couldn't move, and now, she didn't know where the others had been taken, or if they were still alive. Where the hell was she? How was she going to escape?

For a moment, fear and hopelessness threatened to overwhelm her. Kylie had been in some bad situations, but nothing like this.

With her hands restrained and her vision blocked, she couldn't see her way out, physically or figuratively. Her breathing became ragged as she almost hyperventilated.

What was she going to do? How could she help herself? How could she help Mac and the others? This couldn't be the end for them. It just couldn't.

Now was not the time to lose her shit. Forcing back the wave of panic, she rolled onto her side.

"Breathe," she said to herself. "Just breathe."

For several seconds, she drew in breaths and let them out slowly, bringing her heartrate under control. As she calmed, her head cleared, and she struggled to a sitting position.

First things first. She had to get out of the sack covering her head and the ties binding her wrists.

Once she was seated in an upright position, she scooted across the dirt floor, searching for a wall, a chair, anything she could lean against. Within seconds she bumped into a wall.

The rough bricks helped to snag the fabric of her hood, allowing her to scrape it from her head. Once she was free of its mustiness, she sucked in deep breaths and cursed a darkness so complete, she couldn't make out anything. Not a door, window or anything else in the room.

Turning her back to the wall, she scraped the zip-tie across the roughness of a brick. She took off a layer of skin before the plastic tie finally broke, freeing her wrists.

Pushing to her feet, Kylie rubbed at the rawness of her wrists before laying her hands on the wall. Inch by inch, she felt her way around the small room that had a dirt floor and brick walls. The door she'd entered through was the only opening. When she reached up, she could touch the low ceiling. Besides the walls, ceiling and dirt floor there was nothing else in the small room.

If she wanted out, she'd have to leave through the door.

Kylie felt the door for a handle, knob or latch, finding none. When she pushed on it, the door held firm. With nothing to pry it loose, no handle to pull, no lock to pick, she would have to dig her way out of her cell with her bare hands.

Despair hit her square in the gut. What was hardest to accept was that she could do nothing to help Mac, Blade or Josh. Had they been delivered to similar cells?

"Mac," Kylie called out softly and strained to hear his response.

When none came, she tried again. "Mac?" Her voice shook in the silence.

Nothing. Not a single sound.

"Blade? Josh?" she called out, raising her voice a little. No one responded.

"Anyone?" she cried, leaning her forehead against the rough wood door. She'd come to rely on the Deltas to keep her safe. Now, they were in as dire a situation as she was. They might not be around to help her out of this. Which meant she had to figure out some way of extricating herself so she could help them.

Kylie straightened, squared her shoulders and ran her fingers along the edges of the rough-hewn, wooden door, searching for a way to open it. Perhaps she could remove the hinges. Her search revealed that the hinges weren't on her side of the door, nor was the handle. The only way she was getting through that door was if someone opened it from the other side.

Fine. She ran her fingers up the rough wall, bumping into a low ceiling. Maybe she could force her way through the roofing material. She pushed on what felt like material similar to the walls. Scratching at it with her fingernails, she tested the hardness.

The roof and walls weren't going anywhere without a knife, pick or jackhammer. Which left the dirt floor.

Kylie dropped to the floor and dug at the dirt with her hands. It, too, was hardpacked and difficult to move. But it was easier scraping away the dirt than it was to break up the bricks in the walls.

With nothing else to do with her time and the safety of the Deltas on her mind, she dug, inch by inch, breaking her nails and rubbing her fingers raw in the process. At one point, she stood and kicked at the dirt with the heel of her boot, working it loose so that she could move it away with her hands. After what felt like an hour, she'd created a shallow depression in the far corner of her cell. At the rate she was working, she might dig a hole big enough to fit through by the time she turned forty.

She hoped and prayed the guys were having more luck getting free.

A couple hours later, she sat with her back to a wall, her hands aching and hope diminishing with every breath she took. There had to be another way.

Footsteps and voices sounded outside the door.

Kylie sprang to her feet and raced to the door. She pulled off one of her boots and held it in her hands ready to use it as a weapon as soon as the door opened.

MAC DIDN'T COME to until he was dropped onto a hard dirt floor. The jolt brought him back to consciousness with a vengeance. He jerked away and fought to get his feet beneath him.

Someone kicked him in his side. Pain shot through him, making him even angrier at himself and the men targeting them. If his hands were free, he'd take the bastard down and choke the life out of him.

A hand slammed down on his head, and the hood flew off.

Mac blinked and looked up at four men holding AK-47s pointed at him, Josh and Blade. The other two men looked to him. He gave a slight nod, indicating he was okay. Blade and Josh returned the nod. A single lantern provided the only light.

He could have kicked himself for letting the Taliban get the better of him and compromising Kylie's safety. But he didn't have time to berate himself, he had to come up with a way out of this mess and to get to Kylie before Ahktar claimed his revenge on her.

The four men with the AK-47s moved aside to allow a man to walk between them. He wore black robes and a black turban. His thick brows and the scar near his left eye gave his identity away. This man was Ahktar, a Taliban leader Special Operations Forces had been after for months and the brother of the man Kylie had killed.

Mac twisted his hands, fighting the plastic zip-tie binding his wrists. This bastard would kill Kylie for having killed his brother. But killing her wouldn't be the worst he could do to her. He'd make her suffer before she died. He couldn't let any of that happen. He couldn't fail Kylie so completely. And when they got out of this alive, he'd tell her exactly how he felt about her and that he wouldn't let her out of his life ever again.

Kylie was his one and only love. He didn't want to live without her. If it meant they only saw each other two weeks out of the year, he'd be happy he was with her for every second of those two weeks. If crumbs of their lives was all he got, he'd be grateful.

Ahktar crossed his arms over his chest and looked down his hawk-like nose at Mac. "Infidels. You will tell me who you are and why you plague my country."

Mac spit on the man's feet.

The guard beside him kicked him in the side.

Mac bit down hard on his tongue to keep from emitting a sound. He'd be damned if he showed an ounce of weakness to these animals.

Ahktar was known for torturing his victims before he beheaded them and displayed their heads as trophies of his reign of terror. Mac wouldn't go down without a huge fight. Hell, he wouldn't go down.

He narrowed his eyes and focused on his enemy.

He'd get through this, free Kylie and destroy Ahktar, if it was the last thing he did in his life.

First, he had to get his hands free. The better to strangle the bastard with...

Ahktar jerked his head toward two of his men and spoke in Pashto.

The men slipped their weapon straps over their shoulders, freeing their hands.

They advanced on Mac, grabbed him beneath his arms and hauled him to his feet.

Another man grounded his weapon and strode toward Mac. When he reached him, he punched him hard in the gut.

Mac would have doubled over, if he could have. The men on either side of him kept him from doing that. His attacker stood back, looking to Ahktar for further guidance.

Ahktar gave him a sneering nod and a short order in Pashto.

The attacker swung his fist at Mac's face.

Mac moved his head to the side at the last second.

The blow caught him on the side of his left cheek. Pain shot through him. He gritted his teeth and held steady, even when a gray haze threatened to envelop him.

The man swung again, aiming at his nose. Mac turned his head the other way.

Again, the blow missed his nose, but hit his right cheek. More pain shot through his face and head, making his head spin and his vision blur.

He couldn't lose consciousness. Kylie needed him. His teammate and Josh needed him.

Warm, wet liquid oozed down his face.

His tormentor continued to punch him until Mac hung limp between the men holding him up.

Finally, Ahktar spoke.

The hands on his arms released, and Mac stumbled then fell between Josh and Blade.

Blade let loose a string of curses.

The men who'd held up Mac jerked Blade to his feet and proceeded to pound him in the face and belly.

With his hands tied behind his back, Mac could do nothing to stop them.

"Move back," Josh whispered as he lay on his side behind Mac.

Mac scooted backward, moving as stealthily as possible.

With all attention on Blade, none of the

guards could see that Josh was chewing on the plastic band binding Mac's wrists.

A moment later, the zip-tie broke, freeing Mac's hands.

He lay for a moment, reviewing his options. What could one man do against five armed men? Fortunately, three of the armed men were busy working over Blade and didn't have their weapons at the ready. That left Ahktar with his handgun and his guard holding an AK-47. He couldn't be sure how many more men Ahktar had outside the building. It didn't matter. Patience wasn't a quality Mac possessed.

When the man beating Blade hit him in the face yet again, Mac couldn't just lay there and let the torture continue.

He bunched his legs, rolled to his feet and plowed into the one man left holding his weapon in front of him.

That man knocked into Ahktar, sending the Taliban leader flying across the room. The handgun he'd been holding flew from his grip and landed in the shadows.

Mac landed on the guard's back, ripped his weapon from his hands, rolled across the floor and came up, pointing the rifle at Ahktar's face.

Without glancing at the man beating Blade, he bit out, "Let my man go, or I kill your leader."

The men holding Blade froze in place.

"Tell them," Mac growled at the Taliban leader.

Ahktar lay on his back, holding his hands up. "They will kill your friend."

"Then you will die," Mac said. "Tell them to let him go."

For a long moment, Ahktar stared up at Mac through narrowed eyes.

His patience gone, Mac shifted the weapon and pulled the trigger, hitting the ground at Ahktar's feet.

The Taliban leader yelped, jumped back and spoke swiftly in Pashto.

The men holding Blade released him.

Blade staggered forward and righted himself.

"Free him," Mac ordered, pointing the AK-47 at Ahktar's other leg. "Now!"

Again, Ahktar issued an order.

The man who'd been beating Blade and Mac, pulled a knife out of the scabbard on his belt and advanced on Blade.

"If he hurts my man, I'll blow a hole in your leg so big you'll lose it."

Ahktar spoke. His guy with the knife snarled and answered back. The Taliban leader addressed one of the men who'd been holding Blade. That man raised his rifle, pointing it at the man holding the knife.

Blade looked to Mac, then turned his back on the guy who'd been using his face like a punching bag.

The knife sliced right through the plastic zip-tie.

Blade spun and divested his torturer of his weapon, yanked his arm up behind him and pressed the blade to his neck. "You bastard. I should kill you."

"Not until we find Kylie," Mac said. "You and Josh take their rifles, tie them up."

"You think we're just going to walk out of here?" Josh asked as Blade cut the tie holding his wrists.

"We have our 'Get of Jail Card' right here." Mac pointed at Ahktar. "We still have three other limbs to negotiate with, before we put him out of our misery."

Josh and Blade used the turbans the men wore to tie their wrists and ankles.

Once they'd finished securing the leader's

men, they confiscated their weapons. All the while, Mac held his pointed at Ahktar. It would give him great pleasure to blow the Taliban terrorist to hell where he belonged, but they needed him as a hostage. That might be the only way they got out of the Taliban camp alive.

Blade and Josh hauled Ahktar to his feet and pushed him toward the door.

"Take us to the woman," Mac said.

Ahktar shook his head. "I cannot."

Mac pressed the barrel of the AK-47 to the Taliban leader's leg. "Take us."

"I cannot. I don't know where she is."

"You lie," Mac said.

Ahktar snorted. "I cannot tell you what I do not know. I had her brought here, but my leader took her. He will use her as an example as to what will happen to news reporters who kill." The Mullah's eyes narrowed, and his lip rose in a feral snarl. "She will pay for what she did to my brother."

"She did what she had to in order to survive," Mac said.

"She murdered my brother," Ahktar spit out. "My family will be avenged."

"We'll see about that." Mac shoved him

through the door. "You can start by telling your men to hold their fire. My finger is on the trigger, pointing at your hip. If anyone tries to stop us, I will destroy you."

As he passed through the door, the Taliban leader called out in Pashto.

With one hand on Ahktar's shoulder, the other on the AK-47, finger resting on the trigger, Mac followed the man out into the open.

Several Taliban soldiers stood in a semicircle around the building, all holding weapons, mostly AK-47s and a few M4A1 rifles like the ones issued to the US military.

"That's my rifle," Blade said through gritted teeth.

"We don't have time to sort out what belongs to who." Mac poked the barrel of his weapon at Ahktar's hip. "Tell them to lay down their weapons in front of my men." Mac felt the longer they jerked around with Ahktar and his men, the farther away Kylie would be taken.

If Ahktar had told him the truth of her being taken away by his superior.

Dread gnawed at his gut. Though he didn't trust Ahktar to tell the truth, he also didn't doubt that someone had taken Kylie. Instinct told him she wasn't there. If she had been, Ahktar wouldn't have appeared so smug about Kylie being used as an example to warn other journalists.

Which meant he had no idea where Kylie was being taken.

CHAPTER 9

KYLIE STOOD to one side and waited for the door to open, her boot in her hands...ready.

The door opened outward.

A burly-looking guard dressed in black stepped inside, his bushy dark eyebrows forming a V over his nose. He glanced back over his shoulder, saying something in what sounded like Pashto.

Because he was looking back, he didn't see the boot coming at him.

Kylie aimed for the nose, swinging hard and in an upward motion, hoping to break it and drive the cartilage up into his head, making his eyes water so that he couldn't see her.

The crunch of the boot hitting his nose indicated she'd struck gold.

The man cried out, blood spurted and he grabbed his face, cursing in his language.

Another man lunged through the door.

Kylie didn't have time to cock her arm for a second swing. She had to rely on the skills she'd acquired in the Krav Maga course she'd taken for over a year while stateside.

She slammed her palm into the second guard's face, hitting him in the nose, hoping to accomplish much the same scenario as she had with the boot. Only this man's nose didn't break. He grabbed her arm and slung her around, clamping his elbow over her throat.

Kylie stomped on his instep, rammed her elbow into his gut, grabbed the arm around her throat and bent double.

In that final move, she flipped the man over her head. He landed flat on his back, the wind temporarily knocked from his lungs.

She didn't have time to think. Kylie dove for the door, swung it closed and locked it from the outside.

The men inside shouted loud enough that

others would hear and come to see what all the fuss was about.

Kylie didn't plan on being there when they arrived. She ran around the mud and stick hut to the rear and raced past a line of similar huts.

"Mac," she whispered loudly as she passed each one. "Blade? Josh?"

No one answered.

She stopped in front of the hut beside the one she'd escaped and lifted the lever that locked the door in place. She pulled it open and peered into the dark interior. "Mac?"

Rustling sounded and a man wearing ragged clothing crawled toward the opening.

Kylie jumped backward, horrified at his appearance.

His face had been badly beaten. His eyes were bruised and swollen. Dried blood caked beneath his nose.

He said something in Pashto.

Kylie shook her head. "I don't understand." She couldn't wait long. The two men yelling in the hut behind her were bound to draw unwanted attention to her plight.

"Help me," the man spoke in English.

Although she needed to keep moving, she

couldn't leave the man. Kylie bent to help him to his feet.

He struggled but managed to straighten then bowed slightly. "I am Musa."

"Kylie," she said curtly, shooting a glance over her shoulder. "I have to go. I have to find my friends," Kylie said.

"You are American," Musa said.

She nodded. "I am. I was with three other Americans. Do you know where they are?"

He shook his head. "I heard Ahktar's men talk about them. They were dropped off five kilometers south of here to be killed."

Kylie's stomach roiled. "No. I have to get to them. They can't die." Not after she'd reconnected with Mac, not after all those wasted years she could have been with him. Now that they'd been given a second chance, she'd be damned if it was taken away.

"Which way is south?" she asked.

The man glanced up at the star-studded sky, so pure and neutral to the human situation. "I will show you."

Kylie frowned. "Can you make it?"

He nodded. "I have to. If I stay, they will kill me in the morning."

"Why?" she asked. "What did you do?"

"I am a teacher. I dared to teach young girls how to read and write."

"Bastards," Kylie muttered. She slipped her arm around the teacher's waist and draped his over her shoulder. "We have to move fast. They will soon learn of my escape."

Together, they moved through the dark village, trying to keep hidden in the shadows of the low, crudely built huts.

Shouts sounded behind them. An engine roared to life, and headlights blinked on somewhere in the midst of the structures.

As they came to the edge of the village, Musa stopped and removed his arm from around her shoulders. "I am too slow. You must go on without me."

"No way," Kylie said. "You've come this far, you have to go the distance to make sure I don't get lost."

He shook his head. "I can create a diversion. It will give you time to get away."

Kylie stared up at the man, the starlight shining down on his kind eyes. "I can't let you sacrifice yourself. You deserve to live as much or more than I do." She squared her shoulders. "We leave this village together or not at all."

Musa's lips curled upward in a tight smile. "You may be sentencing yourself to death."

"I'll take that chance. I'm not leaving you with them." She picked up the pace, hauling him along with her as fast as she could go with his weight bearing down on her.

As they left the little village, they had to cross an open stretch of ground that left them vulnerable. If the vehicle they'd revved up reached the edge of the village before Kylie and Musa reached cover, their escape would be short-lived.

The Taliban could recapture them or just shoot them in the back. Either way, they'd be dead by morning.

With that in mind, Kylie pushed on when her exhaustion threatened to slow her down.

Running was hard enough alone. With a wounded, beaten man, it was exponentially difficult. Twice they stumbled and almost fell.

"You should leave me," Musa said. "I will continue by myself."

"No," Kylie said through gritted teeth, her lungs and muscles burning with the effort. If they could make it just a little farther, they could hide in the hills, making their way south in more rugged, yet protected terrain.

Kylie had to stop to catch her breath. A glance over her shoulder made her blood run cold and her pulse ratchet up. A vehicle left the village, heading their way.

In the light from the stars above, she could see it was a truck loaded with men. Each man held a rifle in the air, shouting as the truck raced toward them.

"Run," Kylie whispered. "Run!"

She tightened her hold on Musa and half-dragged, half-carried the man toward the hillside south of the village.

"Just a few...more...feet," she gritted out.

She could hear the truck rumbling across the dirt road behind her, the men on board firing their weapons. Whether they were shooting at them or into the air, Kylie couldn't say. She wasn't looking at them. She focused on the hills in front of her, knowing that even if she and Musa reached them before the men in the back of that truck, they still had to climb.

Though her strength waned, she couldn't give up now. They'd come too far. Ahktar wouldn't let her live after killing his brother. He'd make her die a slow painful death.

Hell, she'd rather be shot and killed in her attempt to escape than captured and tortured to death. Ahktar's reputation scared her more than she cared to admit. If she only had a smidgen of a chance to escape, she wasn't going to waste it.

"Come on, Musa," she said, breathing hard, her lungs feeling as if they would explode with as much air as she was forcing through them.

Then they were climbing, up and away from the road. She thought she couldn't catch her breath on the flat ground. Now she was moving on a prayer, her body almost played out, her back aching from taking the bulk of Musa's weight.

Kylie didn't stop, she couldn't. Not now. She had to get away from these men before she could get back to Mac, Blade and Josh. They needed her.

She didn't stop to think that she might need them.

Mac walked Ahktar to the nearest vehicle and stopped.

"Tie him up," he said to Blade.

Blade ripped a strand of fabric from the man's turban to secure his hands behind his back. Then he tied his ankles with the remainder of the turban.

Without the head covering, the man's hair stuck out wildly. He didn't look as intimidating or tough.

Mac knew better. The man was a monster who loved to torture his victims in the most painful ways. He was pure evil. He'd be damned if he let him get away.

"Now, you'll tell me where your boss took Kylie."

Ahktar lifted his chin, his eyes narrowing. "I do not know."

"Which direction did he go when he left?" Mac demanded.

"I do not—"

Mac grabbed the man's arms and raised then up behind him as far as he could.

The man cried out and bent over to ease the pain. He fell on his face since his ankles were secured. "They went north," he said into the dirt.

Mac nodded toward Blade and Josh. "Load him up."

The two men shoved the Taliban leader into

the back seat. Blade climbed in beside him, holding his rifle pointed at the man's head.

"How good are you at driving stick shift?" Mac asked Josh.

"Good," Josh answered.

"You drive," Mac said. "I'll ride shotgun in case we need firepower."

Josh slipped into the driver's seat and started the engine while Mac climbed into the passenger seat. "Let's find Kylie."

Josh fumbled with the shift and popped the clutch.

The SUV lurched forward and died.

Josh swore. "I know how to do this.'"

"Breathe," Mac said. "Now...get us out of here."

Drawing in a deep breath, Josh started the engine, cupped the shift in his palm and moved it into first gear. He eased off the clutch and the vehicle moved forward smoothly.

He handled the rest of the gears as well and soon they were racing north into the night.

The road ran straight for the first two kilometers until they approached a line of hills in their path. They zigzagged through the hills, climbing higher before they topped a ridge and worked their way down the other side.

As the road curved past rocky outcroppings, Mac strained to see the valley ahead.

A light blinked in the distance. Or did it? Mac couldn't be certain. They rounded another rocky bluff area, blocking his view of the valley below.

As they turned back the other direction, Mac saw it again.

The lights belonged to a vehicle on the road at the base of the hill. Every glimpse he managed to catch made Mac more certain the vehicle wasn't moving. It had stopped at the base of the hill, shining the headlights off the road.

His gut knotted. Why would they be shining their lights off the road? Were they were trying to find someone?

"We've got company ahead of us," Josh said. "What do you want me to do?"

"Stop in the next curve. I'll go the rest of the way on foot."

"By yourself?" Josh asked.

Mac's jaw tightened. "Yes."

Blade snorted. "The hell you will."

"We can't leave Ahktar," Mac said.

"Josh can handle him," Blade said.

"What if the two of us run into trouble?" Mac said. "How's Josh going to get to safety?"

"I'll hole up until the rest of your team catches up to us."

"*If* they can find us." Mac shook his head.

"I got off a call when we were stopped in traffic in Kabul," Blade said. "They could get the Intelligence community working on finding us and send help our way."

Mac laughed, without humor. "And pigs could learn to fly."

"I can handle him," Josh said.

"If he causes any problems, shoot him," Blade said.

Josh laughed. "Kylie's the better shot. That's what got us into all this trouble."

"And if she hadn't been a good shot," Mac said, "you wouldn't be here today."

Josh nodded, the smile slipping from him face. "You're right. She's the only reason I'm alive."

"And we need to make sure we're the reason she stays alive herself." Mac nodded toward a bend in the road that had enough room for them to pull off and park the SUV behind a boulder.

Blade climbed out of the back seat, released

the magazine out of the rifle and examined it. "I have about ten rounds."

Mac did the same with his AK-47. "I have about the same."

Josh released his magazine and removed several bullets from it and handed them to Mac. "You might need more than I will. I really only need two. One to shoot Ahktar with, the other in case I miss the first time."

Blade ripped a piece of fabric from what he'd used to tie Ahktar's wrists. He wadded it up and yanked the man's head back and shoved the fabric into the man's mouth. "That way he can't give your position away."

"If we aren't back in two hours..." Mac shrugged. "I'd like to say head back to Kabul, but you don't know who you'll run into on the road. You might be better off waiting here for help to arrive."

"I'll figure out something." Josh waved a hand toward them. "Go. Find Kylie. I'd go with you but..." He jerked his head toward Ahktar. "We can't leave this guy. He's killed to many of our own."

Mac glanced at Blade. "Ready?"

Blade nodded in the starlight. "Let's do this."

"If it's nothing, we'll be back soon. If it's a full can of worms, well..." Mac paused. "Keep your head down. Don't let them know where you are. If you have to leave that bastard, do it. Just don't let the Taliban catch you."

Josh nodded. "Gotcha. Shoot the bastard and run. Seriously, be careful out there. And find Kylie. I hate to think what they'll do to her."

Mac hated to think of that as well. The Taliban weren't known for their kindness to the opposition. They'd sooner cut off your head than sit down to peace talks.

Without another word, Mac and Blade set off down the hill, taking a more direct route than going by the winding road.

They slid down the slopes in their hurry to reach the bottom where the vehicle was shining the headlights into the hillside. When they could, they ran, but for the most part it was a steep slope. All they could do was sit and ride the gravel downward. As they neared the bottom, they heard men shouting in Pashto.

A small rise blocked their view of the vehicle below. When they reached the top, they peered over the edge, keeping their heads down in case they came face to face with their enemy.

Below, flashlights blinked in and out as men climbed the hillside, dropped down into ravines and moved up the other side.

They were headed in Mac and Blade's direction. If they shined their lights higher up the escarpment, they might even catch sight of them.

But they weren't shining the lights higher, they were looking closer to where they were.

What were they looking for?

"I'd give my eye teeth for night vision goggles right now," Blade whispered.

"Yeah," Mac murmured, searching the area in front of the flashlight beams.

The starlight helped some, but whatever they were looking for must be hanging in the shadows or crawling low to the ground. Mac couldn't make out—

"Fuck," Blade said. "Do you see what I see?"

"No. What are they looking for?"

Blade grabbed Mac's head and turned it so that he was looking farther ahead of the men with the flashlights and closer to where they were perched. "Look at that ridge down below us. See that?" Blade pointed.

Mac followed his finger to the ridge Blade indicated. Movement caught his attention. He squinted, trying to make out what it was. "What is it?"

"I'm not sure. Something big. Looks like it has four legs."

The creature stepped into the starlight and Mac sucked in a breath. "It's two people. One holding onto the other. One shorter than the other."

"You think it might be Kylie?" Blade asked.

Mac's jaw hardened and his fists closed around his rifle. "If it is, someone could be holding her hostage. Come on. We have to be sure before we blow our cover." Mac slipped over the top of the ridge, keeping his body as close to the ground to avoid presenting a silhouette target for the Taliban to shoot at.

They had to be stealthy and swift at the same time. On the rugged terrain, that was nearly impossible. Especially when they needed to get to the two people before the men with the flashlights reached them.

The race was on.

CHAPTER 10

KYLIE'S back ached and her legs burned and felt like jelly at the same time. They could hear the shouts of the men below. It wouldn't be long before they caught up with them. Unfortunately, Kylie couldn't keep up the pace. Hell, she could barely stand, and Musa was quickly losing what little strength he'd been able to muster thus far.

The man had been beaten so badly, it was a miracle he was still upright.

At that moment, Musa stumbled, his body lurching forward, taking Kylie down with him.

Once they started to fall, Kylie had no way to keep it from happening. She couldn't take one more step. All she could do was aim to land in the shadow of a large boulder, praying it would provide enough concealment for both of them to remain hidden from the flashlight beams.

Maybe the men below would miss them all together and leave.

Kylie hit the ground on her knees.

Musa landed on one knee and toppled onto his side. He lay so still, Kylie thought he might be dead. She pressed her fingers to the base of his throat, her pulse pounding hard from her rush up the hill.

Before she could feel the man's pulse, a hand came up and Musa whispered. "I am not dead, yet."

"Good," she said so softly, no one but Musa would be able to hear her voice. She grabbed the man's arm and pulled him toward the shadow cast by the giant boulder. "Must hide," she said as she inched him across the ground.

He helped as much as he could. Between the two of them, they were able to scoot, roll and slide into the darkness of the shadow.

Musa lay on his back, his eyes closed.

Even if they weren't being chased by the Taliban, Musa might not make it. He could be suffering from internal injuries caused by the beatings.

Kylie collapsed on the ground beside Musa and dragged in deep breaths, filling her starving lungs with air.

Just when she could breathe normally again, she heard a sound in the darkness.

Instead of it coming from below them, it was coming from above. Loose gravel slithered down the slope behind her, landing at her feet.

Kylie gasped and spun on her haunches in time to see two figures, both carrying guns, sliding down the hillside toward her.

She had no time to react. No time to run before the figures crashed into her and Musa.

Though she was exhausted, Kylie rolled onto her feet and prepared to take on whoever it was who'd plowed into her and her new friend.

"Kylie?" a familiar voice said beside her.

"Mac?" She spun and threw herself into his arms. "Oh, sweet Jesus. Is it really you?"

"Shh, sweetheart." He chuckled softly. "Yes, it's me. And Blade's here as well."

"Josh?"

"Waiting in a vehicle not far from here."

"He's alive?" she asked, tears welling in her eyes. "You're all alive." The tears spilled down her cheeks. She quickly swiped them away, grabbed his hand and pulled him to. Crouching position. "You have to get down. There are men after us."

"I know. I counted a cool dozen," Blade said. "Give or take a few."

The crunch of gravel sounded nearby.

Mac touched a finger to his lips, indicating they should all be silent.

All four of them hunkered low behind the boulder.

Mac stood at one side of the boulder and held his rifle at the ready, aiming toward the sound of footsteps heading their direction.

Blade took up a position on the other side of the boulder, aiming in the direction of the sound.

A moment later, a young Taliban soldier walked by the boulder, shining his flashlight right then left, the beam landing on Mac's face at the same time as Mac grabbed him clamped an arm around his neck and locked him in a chokehold.

The soldier dropped the flashlight and his rifle and clawed at Mac's arm trying to free himself.

Mac's arm flexed as he tightened his hold.

Kylie grabbed the rifle from where it had landed on the ground and assumed Mac's previous position on the edge of the boulder. She couldn't stand by and not do anything. Their lives were at risk. And Mac had found her. Her chest swelled with love and gratitude. Together, they could conquer the world.

MAC'S HEART SWELLED. This woman was smart as well as beautiful.

She knew that, though he'd caught the young man before he could fire a shot or shout, the sound of their scuffle could draw attention.

As if on cue, another man, wielding a flashlight and a rifle appeared on the opposite side of the boulder.

Still contending with the first man, Mac prayed Blade could handle the new threat on his own.

Blade flashed the knife he'd taken from Ahktar's men and dispatched the latest Taliban soldier with little more noise than the clatter of his rifle and flashlight hitting the ground.

The man would no longer be a threat to anyone as he bled out of his torn carotid artery.

Mac's guy finally slumped in his arms. When he released him, the guy sank to the ground.

A quick check for a pulse indicated he was still alive. Mac secured the man's hands with his own belt. Then tearing a piece of fabric from the soldier's loose-fitting outfit, Mac stuffed that wad into his mouth, effectively gagging him, in case he woke before Mac got Kylie out of there.

"We've got more coming," Kylie said. "We're far outnumbered. Any plans for getting out of here alive?" she asked.

Mac shook his head. "Not one." If all four of them left the protection of the boulder, they'd be spotted. Even with two fewer soldiers, they still outnumbered Mac and Blade ten to two. They could attempt to pick them off, one by one until the others got smart and came at them from another direction. Hell, if they circled and came at them from behind, they wouldn't stand a chance.

"Between what ammo we brought with us and the additional weapons we just acquired," Blade said, "we can make it sound like there are more than two of us. Maybe we can scare them off."

"And when the ammunition runs out?" Mac asked.

Blade shrugged. "It was a thought."

"Or we could create a diversion," Kylie offered in hushed tones. "Any way we can blow up their vehicle?"

Mac's mouth twisted. "One of us would have to get there without being detected."

"I'll go," Blade said.

Mac shook his head. "You're better at hand-to-hand combat. You're more likely to take down one of these guys without all the noise of firing a weapon. I'm better at making a lot of noise." Mac pulled Kylie into his embrace and brushed a kiss across her lips. "I'm going."

She held onto his hand. "No."

"I'll draw their attention away from here. Then I'll work my way back to their truck and find a way to make a statement. When their attention is diverted, get back to Josh and the SUV."

"Please," Kylie whispered. "Be careful."

He nodded. "I will be. But I have to do this." After a quick kiss, he left them and eased out from behind the boulder.

At that moment another Taliban soldier appeared, shining his light at a different outcropping.

Mac clamped his arm around the man's neck

and cut off the air to his windpipe to keep him from calling out to his comrades.

Instinctively, the man dropped his rifle and flashlight and grabbed at the arm around his neck with both hands.

Tightening his hold, Mac dragged him back behind the boulder.

Blade was there to gag he man and took over. He secured him, tying his wrists and ankles. "Go," Blade urged. "It won't be long before the others find us here.

Mac left, swinging wide of the line of men with flashlights combing the hillside for Kylie and Musa. He hurried downward, formulating a plan as he went. A couple times on the way down, he chucked a rock toward some of the searchers, making them think they were getting close to their quarry, when, in fact, they were led in the opposite direction.

Most of the men were in the hills. A couple had remained at the truck, guarding it with their AK-47s. But they were looking up at the men conducting the search.

They didn't see Mac as he circled around and came up from behind. The truck doors hung open. He thought about lighting a rag and sticking it in the gas tank, but he didn't have a match or lighter to create a flame.

As the two men stood near the front of the vehicle, their backs to him, Mac slipped into the driver's seat. Taking a deep breath, he twisted the key in the ignition, praying it would start on the first try. He wouldn't get another chance.

The engine turned over and engaged.

The two men in front of him spun, their eyes wide.

Mac pointed his gun out the window and fired at them, forcing them to dive to the ground. At the same time he shifted into first gear and stomped on the accelerator. The doors on each side slammed shut as the vehicle leaped forward.

The men on the ground rolled to get out of the way of the oncoming truck. By the time they got up, Mac had the truck heading toward a rocky escarpment at full speed.

Bullets slammed through the back windshield, spraying glass into the cab.

Mac ducked low and kept going, increasing the speed as he bumped over rough terrain.

At the last moment, he gunned the accelerator, flung open the driver's door and threw himself out. Hitting the ground hard, he tucked his arms and legs and rolled away from the racing vehicle.

The truck slowed as soon as his foot left the accelerator, but not soon enough to stop it from crashing into the bluff.

A moment later, the gas ignited, shooting a column of flame into the sky.

Mac lay for a moment in the ravine, knowing that if he stood, he would be silhouetted against the fire and make an easy target for the Taliban. And if all went according to his plan, they would be heading toward him and away from Kylie and the others.

Low-crawling to the top of the ditch he'd landed in, he blinked to adjust his night vision after being blinded by the light of the flame still burning behind him.

For a moment, he could see nothing but blackness. But as he studied the hillside he'd come down from, he could see the silhouettes of men hurrying back down to investigate the crash of their only mode of transportation.

He let go of the breath he'd been holding. His plan to distract them had worked. Before he could break his arm patting his own back, he realized he would soon be surrounded by Taliban soldiers.

With the bluff behind him, he didn't have many avenues of escape. He could really use a miracle to get him out of the situation alive.

As the roar of the fire faded, Mac could hear another sound that gave him hope...the thumping rumble of rotors beating the air grew louder.

Mac looked to the sky. Two Black Hawk helicopters sped toward them.

Could it be possible his team had found them?

A miracle he'd needed. Now one winged its way toward him.

All he had to do was stay alive long enough for the people in that chopper to rescue him from the bloodthirsty men converging on the crashed vehicle and his position.

He crawled along the shallow ravine, heading away from the fire, staying low to the ground.

As the chopper neared, the Taliban soldiers slowed and looked up at the sky.

"That's right," Mac murmured to himself. "Focus on them, not me. They're bringing a whole lot of whoop ass on your heads."

At least he hoped that was why they were there and not on their way to another engagement.

One moment he could see the choppers in the sky, the next they'd disappeared.

His hope for a rescue drained.

If he wanted to live, he had to save his own ass.

CHAPTER 11

Kylie followed Mac until he disappeared, praying that wouldn't be the last time she saw him alive.

Then she turned to guard her side of the boulder. She didn't have a knife or the same kind of strength to subdue a man without creating a whole lot of noise. Yes, she knew Krav Maga, but those techniques were defensive. She would have to go into offensive mode to protect Musa and Blade.

As she waited for whatever diversion Mac had in mind, she spotted the blink of a flashlight headed toward her side of the boulder.

Kylie tensed and prepared to shoot rather than be shot. Pulling the trigger had been what got her into this mess in the first place. But, like the first time, it was kill or be killed. Blade and Musa relied on her to protect them.

Raising her rifle, she aimed at the figure heading her way, holding her fire until absolutely certain it was the only alternative.

As the man inched forward, Kylie drew in a deep breath and held it, sighting her weapon on her target, her finger moving from the trigger guard to the trigger, resting lightly on the cool metal.

Then a loud crash was followed by a burst of flame lighting the sky.

The man in front of her spun toward the commotion. Moments later, he ran back the way he'd come, heading for the fire and away from Kylie, Blade and Musa.

Kylie released the breath she'd been holding and removed her finger from the trigger, slumping over the rifle.

What had Mac managed to explode in his successful diversion? And had he managed to get out of the way in time?

"Come on, now's our time to get away." Blade bent to loop Musa's arm over his shoulder. "The Taliban are headed toward the explosion."

"What about Mac?" Kylie asked. Now that they could leave, she didn't want to.

"He'll find his way back," Blade said. "He's a cat with a lot of lives left to live." He started up the hill. "Cover me until we get over that ridge."

Because she couldn't abandon Blade and Musa, Kylie followed, backing up the hill, aiming her rifle downward in case some of the Taliban soldiers had chosen to continue their search instead of investigating the explosion.

No one stopped them. They were all headed toward Mac and the fire blazing high into the sky.

Kylie's heart contracted as they slipped over the top of the ridge and out of sight of the crash scene below. She should have felt relief but didn't. How could she when the man she loved was down there somewhere, possibly surrounded by Taliban.

A thumping sound filled the air.

"Hallelujah," Blade exclaimed. "Black Hawks! Hopefully they're coming for us."

Hope surged in Kylie's chest. "If they are, we don't have to leave Mac. We need to go back and cover for him until help arrives."

Blade frowned in the starlight. "If I know

Mac, he'd rather know you were safe and out of harm's way."

"I can't go," Kylie said. "You two go on without me. I'm heading back to help Mac."

"You don't have to go it alone. Looks like the choppers are landing in that depression ahead." Blade tipped his head toward the helicopters, dropping low into the hills, choosing a flat spot to set down. As soon as they landed, men streamed out of the sides.

"Stay here with Musa," Blade commanded as he eased Musa to the ground. "I'll make the connection and lead them back this way."

Before Kylie could protest, Blade took off across the rugged terrain. He met up with the soldiers coming off the helicopters. In seconds, they were headed back to Kylie and Musa's position.

Blade stopped long enough to let Kylie know what was happening. "It's our Delta Force team," he said with a grin. "They're going in to bring Mac back. I'm taking a couple of them with me to relieve Josh of Ahktar. You'll need to come with me."

"I want to go with the others to help Mac," Kylie said.

Blade shook his head. "You'll only slow them down. If you want to help Mac, stay with me."

Kylie watched as the team ran across the terrain, fresh for the fight, unlike her. They would get there much faster than if she went with them.

"If you go with them, their focus will be on protecting you, not on getting to Mac," Blade argued.

Kylie squeezed her eyes shut for a second, then opened them and squared her shoulders. "Okay. I want them to get to Mac as quickly as possible. Lead the way to Josh. I'll follow."

Between Blade and his buddy Dash, they half-carried Musa down the hill and back up the other side. Just when Kylie thought they'd never get to Josh and Ahktar, they rounded a boulder near a gravel road and came upon an SUV.

A voice called out, "Halt! Who goes there?"

"Josh, it's me, Blade and we have Kylie."

Josh stepped out of the shadows, leveling the rifle on Blade. Then he pointed the weapon toward the ground. "I thought you'd never make it back. And when I heard that explosion..." He shook his head as smile cross his lips as he spied Kylie. "Thank God."

Kylie ran to him and threw her arms around his neck. "I was so worried about you."

"Same here. I'm glad they found you." He looked up from her face and frowned at Dash and Musa. "You're not Mac. Where's Mac?"

Kylie's eyes filled with tears. "The Deltas are going in to bring him out."

"He's not...dead?" Josh asked.

Kylie shook her head. "No. He can't be."

"We don't know. The team will get him out. In the meantime, how's our prisoner?"

"He tried to get out of his bindings, but they held. And I didn't take the gag out of his mouth." Josh's lips twisted. "I didn't get to shoot him."

Kylie laughed. "You sound disappointed."

"The bastard would have killed you," Josh said, a frown forming a V with his eyebrows.

"I'm alive." She turned back the way she'd come and stared into the darkness. "Now all we need is Mac to come back alive."

For the next twenty minutes, she wrung her hands, pacing back and forth in front of the SUV, her attention on the hills she'd passed through to get where she now waited.

When she heard the sound of rotor blades

beating the air, her heart leaped into her throat and she turned to Dash.

Dash laid a hand over his ear, a smile spreading across his face. "They have Mac." His grin broadened. "He's alive and asking about you."

The rush of relief that washed over Kylie was so powerful, it sent her to her knees. Tears filled her eyes and spilled down her cheeks.

"Hey," Blade slipped an arm around her waist and drew her to her feet. "He's alive, not dead."

"I know," she said. "I'm just so happy."

Blade laughed. "That's a funny way of showing it."

Dash frowned. "We need to drive down the mountain into the open so the choppers can pick us up."

Kylie didn't have to be told twice. They piled into the SUV and raced back out of the hills in the opposite direction from the fire and the Taliban. When they came out into the flat lands, one of the helicopters had landed. The other hovered nearby.

Josh drove the SUV to within a few yards of the helicopter. Kylie leaped out of her seat and ran for the bird.

Mac climbed out and held his arms open for her.

She ran into them and hugged him so tightly, she didn't think she would ever let go.

Finally, he kissed the top of her head and said, "We need to get in, or they'll leave us."

Blade and Dash helped Musa into the chopper. Rucker and Bull got Ahktar in and buckled him into a harness.

Soon they were flying through the air, away from the Taliban.

Kylie sat beside Mac, holding his hand, thanking God for saving the only man she'd ever loved.

WITHIN FORTY MINUTES, they were landing at Bagram Airfield where they disembarked from the helicopters onto the tarmac.

Glad to see the safety of the base, Kylie was sad to know she'd be separated from Mac all too soon.

Rucker met them at the edge of the landing zone where a couple of SUVs were waiting. "We called ahead. They have a plane leaving in a less than an hour. We can get Kylie and Josh on it, if we hustle."

The Military Police took charge of Ahktar and loaded him into one of the SUVs.

"They'll take him to the intelligence guys," Rucker said. "The main thing is that he's out of commission and no longer torturing our people."

"What about Musa?" Kylie asked.

Rucker smiled. "We're working on that. I've put him in touch with the state department. We're trying to get him asylum to the US. In the meantime, they'll keep him safe. Right now, you need to get to the terminal and get processed through."

They hurried to the air transportation office to fill out the necessary paperwork to get them booked onto the next flight, leaving in less than an hour.

The Deltas stayed with Kylie and Josh. Rucker worked on getting transportation back to their forward operations base, while Mac helped Josh and Kylie wade through the documents they had to fill out and sign.

When Kylie had all the documentation completed, she waited for the loadmaster to wave her and Josh through. She waited with

Mac, struggling to find the words that would make them right with each other. She couldn't think of anything but the truth.

"I want to see you again," she blurted out.

"Can I see you again?" Mac asked at the same time.

Kylie laughed and stepped into his arms. "Is it crazy to think we could have a second chance at this?"

"Define *this*," he said.

"Us."

He nodded and brushed a strand of her hair back from her forehead, tucking it behind her ear. "That would be a *yes* from me. What are you feeling?"

"One hundred percent relieved," she said with a breathy laugh.

His brow wrinkled. "Not exactly the words I was looking for."

"Relieved that you think we have a chance. Because I want it so badly."

"Not half as bad as I do," he said and nuzzled her neck. "I've dreamed of holding you just like this for so long, I think I might still be dreaming."

"Same here," she said, wrapping her arms around his neck. "You're at Fort Hood, right?"

He nodded.

"Any idea when you'll be back?" she asked.

"Whenever they're done with us here," he said. "How long that will be, I have no idea."

"Is it possible for two people with careers like ours to make a relationship work?" she whispered. *Please, say yes.*

"If both parties are equally committed, I think so." He tipped her chin up. "I'm that committed."

"Miss Adams, Mr. Bolton, it's time to board the plane," a voice called out.

Kylie had so much more she wanted to say, but they were out of time. "I'm that committed, too," she said, holding his gaze.

"Miss Adams, Mr. Bolton?" the voice called out again.

Josh started toward the exit, stopped and turned back. "Kylie, they're waiting on us."

"I have to go." Kylie wrapped her arms around his neck and kissed him.

Mac crushed her to him and held her tight.

She wished she could stay, but the time had come to leave. Kylie slipped her backpack over one of her shoulders and hurried away, her eyes blinded by the tears falling freely.

She was almost to the door when a hand on

her arm stopped her.

"You'll need this," Mac's voice said in her ear.

She glanced up through her tears.

He pressed a napkin into her hand, closed her fingers around it and sent her on her way.

It wasn't until she was seated on the airplane that she opened her hand and stared down at the napkin. Inside, written in Mac's bold handwriting were the words *I Love You.* Beneath it was his phone number.

She laughed and cried all at once. Mac never said anything he didn't mean.

He loved her.

And she loved him. She smiled as she held the napkin to her chest. It wasn't as good as holding Mac, but it would have to do until she could get back to the States and make a few changes.

The first being her place of residence. She was moving from Dallas to Killeen, the town outside of Fort Hood. Hopefully, she could make that happen before Mac returned from Afghanistan. If not, it would be soon after.

She couldn't wait to start her new life with the only man she'd ever loved. What that life would be like was a huge question but one she was willing to find the answer to.

CHAPTER 12

"YOU GONNA LOOK up your girl, now that you're back?" Dash asked Mac.

Mac grabbed his duffel bag and turned on his phone for the first time in days, glad to be off the plane and back in Texas.

"She didn't give me her phone number," he said.

"What? All that face sucking, and she doesn't want to see you again?"

Mac had worried for the past week, wondering if he'd been stupid. Why hadn't he asked her for her phone number?

He'd given her his. If it was meant to be, he'd hear from her. "It was her move," he said.

"Uh, I think it's your move, now," Dash said.

Turning with his duffel bag in his hand, Mac was confronted with a huge poster decorated with bright green glitter and the words, *I LOVE YOU, MAC*, written in large, bold letters.

He couldn't see who was holding it, only the sexy, bare legs beneath the poster board.

His heart slammed hard against his ribs and beat so fast he could barely breathe.

He strode to the poster board, dropped his duffel on the ground and lowered the board to see the face that had been on his mind since he'd watched her walk out to the plane at Bagram Airfield.

"Kylie," he said on a sigh and gathered her to him. "How did you know I'd be here?"

"I have my contacts." She laced her hands behind his neck and pulled him down to her. "Did you like my sign?"

He nodded and kissed the tip of her nose. "The sweetest words I've ever seen in green glitter."

"I wanted to make sure you saw it," she said, tears pooling in her eyes. "I love you, Mac. And if you'll have me, I want to be with you always.

Well, at least when I'm in the country and you are, too."

"I want that more than you can possibly know," he said.

Her brow furrowed. "There's something I wanted to ask you." She stepped back until his hands had to fall to his sides.

Then she dropped to one bare knee, the hem of her sun dress brushing the floor. "Sean McDaniel, I love you, which we've already established, and I want to be with you always. Sean 'Mac' McDaniel, will you marry me?" She lifted the poster board and turned it around. In shiny pink glitter were the big, bold words, *PLEASE SAY YES.*

Mac laughed, took the poster from her hands, tossed it to the side and then answered with all of his heart.

"A thousand times, *yes!*"

Rucker, Dash, Blade, Tank, Bull, Dawg and Lance let out a hearty cheer and pounded him on the back.

"Congratulations, Mac," Rucker said. "She's a keeper. She'll have your back, no matter the situation."

"Yeah, man," Dash said. "And if you screw this up, I'll be there to help her pick up the pieces."

Mac glared at Dash. "I'm not going to screw it up. You can't have Kylie."

Dash held up his hands. "It doesn't hurt to throw my hat in the ring. Just saying."

"A woman after my own heart," Dawg said. "Never met a woman who scored three kills." He shook Mac's hand and hugged Kylie.

"You're a lucky bastard," Tank said. "Be nice to her. She's amazing."

"I know."

"Better marry her before she comes to her senses," Bull warned.

"I will," Mac said. "How's next week sound?" he asked Kylie.

"I'm all in," she said. "The sooner we start our lives together, the happier I'll be."

Mac crushed her to him and kissed her until they both ran out of breath. "I love you, Kylie, and I'm not letting you get away this time."

"I promise. I'm not going anywhere," she said. "You're the one who completes me."

He chuckled, happier than he'd ever been. "And you're the only woman for me."

THE END

Interested in more military romance stories?
Subscribe to my newsletter and receive the
Military Heroes Box Set
Subscribe Here

BREAKING FREE

TAKE NO PRISONERS BOOK #1

New York Times & *USA Today*
Bestselling Author

ELLE JAMES

BREAKING Free

New York Times & USA Today Bestselling Author

ELLE JAMES

CHAPTER 1

"I STILL DON'T UNDERSTAND why I got stuck with the job," Bull said.

Rucker pounded him on the back. "It's because you're the biggest, best looking guy on the team. Most of all, you know what manners are. The rest of us are clueless."

"I should never have told any of you that my mother sent me to a cotillion," Bull muttered.

"Got that right," Dash said. "That just opens you up to a whole lot of grief."

"Here, let me take a look at you." Blade stood in front of Bull and adjusted his collar. "I don't understand why they're not sending *me* in."

"Are you kidding?" Mac shook his head. "You

think you're some kind of ladies' man. You'd be screwing every female in there."

"I'm not some horndog looking for a little tail." Blade grinned. "I'm a little more selective than that."

Rucker laughed. "Not much. Still...while Bull's eating steak and drinking wine with the hot shots, we'll be stuck bunking with each other, eating MREs."

"Not necessarily," Dash said. "We have our cover, too. We're supposed to be a mix of contractors and tourists, so we'll get a chance to sample some of the local cuisine."

"Yeah," Blade said, "but it won't be steaks like they'll be having at the embassy."

Bull would rather have stayed with the other guys. Being the lone man on the inside wouldn't be as much fun. "What exactly is my job inside?"

"To keep us informed," Rucker said. "The ambassador will fill you in when you get inside. It's supposed to be super-secret, just between us and him."

Bull swallowed a groan. Great, he'd probably be babysitting the ambassador the entire time. And he wouldn't be allowed to take in his M4A1 rifle. "Can I take *any* kind of weapon?"

"Maybe a pocketknife but *no* guns," Rucker said. "That's why we're sending in the biggest guy. You're the best one at hand-to-hand combat. You can take down just about anybody inside that compound. Hopefully, you won't have to though."

Blade grinned. "Look at you, all dressed up. You almost look like a civilian." He stood in front of Bull, straightened the collar once more on the button-down dress shirt, adjusted the necktie and ran his gaze from top to toe. "Look pretty good to me. That cotillion practice did you some good."

Bull tugged at the knot at his neck. "I hate neckties."

"Consider it like you're taking one for the team," Dash said.

"Yeah, yeah," Bull muttered and glanced down at his watch. "Damn. I've only got fifteen minutes to get inside the compound to be on time for my meeting with the ambassador."

"Better get going," Rucker said. "You know where we'll be for the most part. You have your cellphone in case you need to get in touch with us, and a radio, should the cellphone get compromised."

Bull patted the pockets on his suit and grabbed the handle of his black, wheeled suitcase.

"Now, remember your name is Greg Smith," Rucker reminded him.

"Greg Smith," he repeated.

"You have everything?" Rucker asked.

Bull patted the fake passport in his pocket and glanced down at his suitcase. "I think so."

"The guard at the gate should let you in, no problem." Rucker stood back and looked him over. "Let's go through the checklist. Passport.

Bull patted his right pocket. "Check."

"Cellphone."

Bull dug in his left pocket. "Check."

"Radio headset in your ears now."

A hand to his ear confirmed Bull had the earbuds in place. "Check."

"Formal wear."

Bull touched the handle of his suitcase "Inside the suitcase. Check."

"Dress shoes?"

Again, he tapped the suitcase. "Also, inside the suitcase. Check."

"Condoms," Blade piped in with a grin.

Rucker back-handed Blade in the belly. "He's going in on a job, not to play."

"Never go anywhere without them." Blade crossed his arms over his chest. "If you're a good boy scout, you're always prepared."

Bull didn't mention that he'd been an Eagle Scout, nor did he mention that he did have condoms packed in his shaving kit. Only because they were already there. Not because he thought he'd need them.

Rucker clapped his hands together. "You're ready. The taxicab will pick you up in front of the hotel across the street in T-minus-two minutes. You'd better get on down there."

"I expect an extraction operation if things get terminally dull," Bull said.

"Ha," Rucker said. "I'm sure you'll find something interesting to keep you from being bored."

Dash chuckled. "You'll just have to deal with it and drink tea with your pinky sticking out."

"I don't drink tea," Bull growled.

"Well, you may have to suffer a little while you're inside. If you're entertaining Turks, they like their tea."

"I'd rather have a beer." Bull would give anything for one at that very moment. He'd chug it for that little bit of buzz it would give him. It might take the edge off.

"You'll have to draw on your cotillion experience," Rucker said. "That's why you're the chosen one."

"Thanks, Mom," Bull muttered beneath his breath. He tugged once more at the tie around his neck and nodded. "I'm ready."

"Break a leg, cowboy," Dash called out.

Rucker clapped him on the back. "Remember to report in once you've settled in and gotten your assignment."

"Roger." Bull left the hotel through a side entrance, circled the block, crossed the street and came back to the hotel where the taxicab was waiting for him. He entered the side of the hotel and came out the front. The taxi was there, waiting, the driver standing by the rear door.

Bull handed him the address for the U.S Embassy, stashed the suitcase in the trunk and climbed into the backseat of the taxi. The embassy was barely a block away and within sight of the hotel where his buddies would be *roughing* it.

In the blink of an eye, the taxi pulled in front of the U.S. Embassy.

"I'll walk from here." He paid the driver and got out of the cab. At the gate, he presented his passport. The guard checked it thoroughly, had him load his suitcase into an x-ray scanner and directed him to walk through the body scanner. The scanner went off and the guard made him back out.

"Sir, please place your cellphone, keys and anything else in the tray, and then go back through."

He emptied his pockets into a tray then walked back through the scanner. He worried that the radio headset might set it off, but he went through without a warning beep.

"Sir, please follow me." One of the guards led him to the embassy building and left him at the front reception desk.

"May I help you, sir?" A woman dressed in a conservative navy skirt suit glanced up over the top of her glasses. "Do you have an appointment?"

Bull nodded. "I do. With Ambassador Grey."

"One moment, sir." She checked his passport, nodded, and then hit the button on the phone in front of her. A couple minutes later, a man in a business suit emerged from an elevator and strode across to the reception desk.

"Mr. Smith, if you'll come with me, I'll take you to the ambassador."

He followed the man into the elevator, and it rose to the top floor. They exited and walked down a hallway to an office. A middle-aged secretary with brown hair and wire-rimmed glasses manned the desk outside the office. She glanced up with a welcoming smile. "Good afternoon, Mr. Smith."

His escort stepped back, turned and walked away.

"You can leave your suitcase here." The secretary pointed to the side of her desk then motioned toward a door. "Ambassador Grey will see you right away."

He parked the suitcase next to her desk and walked through the door. A tall man with graying hair stood up from behind his desk and crossed the room with his hand held out. "Mr. Smith, so glad you could come."

He took the man's hand in a firm grip. "Nice to meet you, Ambassador Grey."

"Please, have a seat." The ambassador

motioned toward a conference table in the corner of the room. He went back to his desk and punched a button on his phone. "Ms. Moore, could you call her one more time? Thank you." He shook his head as he walked across to the conference table and sat in the chair at the end. "I appreciate you and your team getting here so fast."

"Yes, sir. What exactly do you want us to do while we're here?"

"As you know, the government in Turkey isn't as stable as it once was. The president has made it more of a military state than a democracy. There have been multiple uprisings, making it more and more dangerous for diplomats, their families and tourists. I'm concerned about my staff. I don't believe the security details assigned to the embassy are enough. They're doing a good job, but if the embassy were stormed, there's no way we would be able to fend off a large-scale attack."

"Sir, the addition of my team might not be enough either."

The ambassador nodded. "I understand that. What I want from your team on the outside is an early warning. And anything they can do to slow down an attack or get my people out before such an assault."

Bull nodded. That was the briefing the Delta Force team had been given.

"As for you," the older man drew in a deep breath and let it out. "I have an entirely different assignment."

Bull's brow furrowed. "Sir?"

The door to the ambassador's office burst open, and a dark-haired young woman rushed in. "Sorry, ambassador," she said as she hurried across to sit in one of the chairs at the conference table. "I had the driver make a detour on my way back from the elementary school. We stopped at the shopping mall so that I could pick up a gift for Ms. Moore's birthday." Once she'd settled in her seat, she glanced across at Bull and then back at the ambassador. "What's this meeting all about?"

The ambassador turned to Bull. "Layla, this is Greg Smith. Mr. Smith, my daughter Layla. She will be your assignment."

Layla glanced from Bull back to the ambassador. "Wait...what?"

Bull blinked. "Sir?"

"That's right, Mr. Smith. Your job inside the

embassy is to gather intel wherever you can, but your number one priority will be looking after the safety and security of my daughter, Layla."

"But, Daddy," Layla said, "I don't need a bodyguard. I already have a couple of guards who follow me around."

"And you keep losing them," the ambassador said with a frown.

Her dark eyebrows swooped downward. "I can't help it they can't keep up with me."

"Your previous guards couldn't go with you everywhere," her father said, "and that's how you were getting away from them."

"I wasn't intentionally trying to lose them," Layla said.

Her father gave her a tight-lipped glare. "Things are getting a little bit too volatile around here for you to be out on the streets by yourself."

Layla leaned back in her seat. "What about sergeants Mitchell and Ramirez? Are you firing them?"

The ambassador shook his head. "They'll still be assigned as your escorts when you leave the embassy compound."

Layla's frown deepened. "You're telling me that I'm to have *three* bodyguards now as I leave the embassy compound? Do you know how hard it is to get three people into a cab? Now I'm going have to get four into a cab?"

"You'll have to make do. And as part of his intelligence gathering function, Mr. Smith will be by your side at every event—dinners, socials and balls."

"How am I supposed to perform my social functions when I have a bodyguard standing next to me?"

"I've thought about that." Her father smiled. "We will present Mr. Smith as your fiancé, not your bodyguard. Your fiancé will be invited to all the functions and all the gatherings, without question. He'll sit at the table with you, stand beside you in receiving lines and basically be your shadow everywhere you go."

Layla rolled her eyes and groaned. "Seriously, Daddy? I'm a grown woman. I don't need a babysitter. Haven't I functioned as your hostess without fail?"

He nodded and laid his hand across his daughter's. "I'm not questioning your ability. I'm just concerned about your safety."

"Daddy, I don't need another bodyguard."

His lips firmed. "The decision has been made.

If you are to stay here at the embassy, you will accept Mr. Smith's protection without question. If you can't do that, then I need to put you on the next plane home."

Layla leaned toward her father. "Daddy, you need me here."

"I don't need you here if it means risking your life." His brow dipped, and his voice deepened. "If the situation gets any hotter, I *will* send you home."

She snorted. "Home? And where might that be? You sold the house I grew up in. We don't have a home back in the United States."

"Home *is* the United States," he said.

"I have more family here in Turkey than I do back in the US."

"Your mother's relatives don't recognize you as part of their family. They disowned her when she married me. What makes you think that they would accept you in their homes?"

Layla frowned. "I'm working on that."

"You do that," the ambassador said, "as long as you take Mr. Smith with you and stay off the streets when the riots start." He looked from Bull to Layla and back to Bull. "I suggest the two of you come up with a cover story for your engagement." He fished a small square box out of his pocket and handed it to Bull. "This was Layla's mother's engagement ring. I had it sized to fit Layla's finger. As of this moment, the two of you are officially engaged."

Bull's gut knotted. "Sir, I'm not sure I want to be a part of this. I'm a soldier, not an actor."

The ambassador chuckled. "Trust me, Mr. Smith, you're going to need every bit of your army training, especially your Delta Force skills, to stay up with my daughter. And to keep her safe."

The ambassador pushed back from the table. "The people in this room are the only three people who will know that this engagement isn't real. That it's a cover. You're not to share that information with anybody else, except maybe your team, if they need to know. But they can't share that information with anyone else." He stared at his daughter. "And you'll make it look real. I've assigned Mr. Smith to the room beside yours, Layla. The closer he is to you the better he can accomplish the job of keeping you safe."

"But Daddy, the embassy is surrounded by guards."

He nodded. "And they're doing an admirable

job," he agreed. "But we've seen what's happened in other countries where embassies are attacked. They can be quickly overwhelmed by numbers. I want to know that you're going to be safe. That the man in charge of your security can get you the heck out of here if the walls are breached."

Layla frowned. "Do you know something that you're not telling me?"

Her father's eyes narrowed. "You know the situation here. The government is run by a president who would make himself dictator. The people aren't happy. The military is keeping them from staging an uprising. I think it's only a matter of time before there's rioting in the streets. And as you well know, not everybody is pro-American. So, humor me," her father said. "Play along with this charade, at least until the political environment calms down a bit." He nodded toward Bull. "I'm counting on you to keep my daughter safe."

Bull nodded, his chest and gut tight. "Yes, sir."

"Now if you'll excuse me, I have a meeting to attend." The ambassador spun on his heel and walked out of the room.

Layla stared across the table at Bull. "I don't

plan on slowing down so that you can keep up with me."

Bull nodded. "Understood." He opened the ring box and stared down at a beautiful black sapphire and diamond ring. "Keep in mind that it might be strange if people see you dodging your fiancé."

She snorted. "You're not my fiancé. We're not engaged."

"According to your father's script, we are." He shoved the ring box toward her. "Do you need a formal declaration of my commitment to protect you?"

"No," Layla said. "I most certainly do not."

"Look, it's not like I *want* to be engaged to you. You're not even my type."

She frowned. "And what's wrong with my type?"

"Nothing if a guy likes a spoiled little rich girl."

"Spoiled little..." She clamped her lips shut and glared at him. "Look, I'm not spoiled. I work hard for my father, and I'm not even paid for it. I do it because I love him, and he needs the support of somebody to perform the functions that a wife normally would."

"And what about your mother?" he asked.

Layla's gazed dropped to the ring box. "My mother died of cancer the year my father was assigned as ambassador to Turkey."

"I'm sorry to hear that," Bull said. He understood how cancer could ravage a person and the family. "What kind of cancer?"

"Pancreatic cancer," she said. "From diagnosis to death was only six weeks." She glanced up, her eyes glassy with unshed tears. "My dad went from her funeral to an airplane to fly to Turkey. I couldn't let him do it alone."

His chest tightened. He wasn't good with female tears. "What about your job?"

"My father's work became my job." She lifted the ring in the box. "She was a really good woman. She made my father very happy. Her family could never understand why she married him, and pretty much cut her off."

"Then why did your father accept a position of ambassador to the country she was raised in?"

"They both hoped that they could work things out with her family. But after my mother's death, my father wasn't as willing to work with her family. He knew how much it broke her heart that they'd cut her off."

"I'm sorry about your mother. I lost my mother to cancer as well. She was far too young to leave this world."

Layla nodded. "Mine, too. She had a lot left to accomplish and never got around to it. She loved her husband, she loved her new country, but she loved her home as well."

Bull couldn't say that he was happy about his assignment, but it was his assignment and he needed to execute it. "Look," he said, "like it or not, we're stuck with each other. We need a cover story, and you need to put this ring on your finger. Where would you like to say we met?"

"I don't care. Pick a spot."

"It has to be some place that you've actually been."

"And you," she said. "Have you ever been to New York City?"

He shook his head.

"How about Miami, Florida?"

Again, he shook his head.

She cocked a single eyebrow. "San Diego?"

He shook his head.

"I went to school at Yale. Any chance you're familiar with Yale?" she asked.

"No," he said.

"Well, where have you been?"

"I grew up near San Antonio, Texas. Have you been there?"

She shook her head. "Good grief, there has to be at least one place that we've both been. What about high school? Where'd you go to high school?"

"In Texas."

"Vacation?"

"Cancun, Mexico?" he suggested.

She shook her head.

"Myrtle Beach, South Carolina?"

Her eyes widened. "I've been there."

"Okay, we've picked a place where we met. We met at Myrtle Beach, South Carolina."

"That was painful," Layla said. "At this rate, we won't have a full backstory until sometime next year. Like when did you propose?"

"I came here to ask your father for your hand in marriage, and then turned around and proposed to you." He took the ring box, got down on one knee and held it out in front of her. "Layla Grey, would you do me the honor of becoming my fiancée for the duration of this assignment?"

Her lips twitched, and the light danced in her eyes. When her lips spread into a smile, the look on her face hit Bull square in the chest.

She held out her ring hand. "Why, Mr. Smith, because my father told me I had to, I accept your offer for the duration of your assignment."

He took the ring from the box and slid it on her ring finger. "I guess then it's official. We got engaged here in your father's office, because you couldn't stand to be apart from me any longer. Ever since we met at Myrtle Beach, South Carolina. How long ago?"

"A year and a half," she answered. "It was our last vacation with my mother."

He nodded. "I could have been there."

"Good, now that that's done…" She pushed to her feet. "I need to get ready for dinner."

He fell in step beside her as she headed for the door. "Since you know where your room is, and my room is next to yours, I'll follow you."

Layla frowned, stopped and faced him. "Just because we're engaged, doesn't mean that you get to take any liberties."

He smiled. "And what kind of liberties would those be?"

Her brow formed a V over her nose. "You

know what I'm talking about."

"I don't know," he said, a smile fighting to be free on his lips. "I'm just a dumb soldier. Maybe you'd better spell it out for me."

Her eyes narrowed. "Suffice it to say...hands off."

He held up his hands. "I told you, you're not my type. I usually go for blondes."

She touched a hand to her dark hair. "Well, that should make it easier then."

He nodded. "I'm not at all interested in you, so you don't have to worry." He cocked a brow. "Don't forget though, we're a newly engaged couple. We have to make everything look real."

"How so?" she asked.

He straightened, towering over her. "I would assume a newly engaged couple would at least hold hands."

Her brow puckered. She thought about it. "I guess that'll be all right."

He moved closer. "A newly engaged man would put his arm around his fiancée like this." He placed his hand at the small of her back.

"Don't push it, soldier," she warned.

His hand fell to his side. "We'll work on that."

"When we're alone," she said, "there's no need

for us to pretend. We can be ourselves."

He nodded. "But when we're in company, we'll have to show a little bit of that PDA."

"PDA?" she asked, her dark eyebrow arching delicately.

"Public display of affection," he clarified.

"I don't know about that," she said.

He held out his hands. "You want people to buy into this charade, don't you?"

"Not really," she replied. "It's my father's idea."

"You don't want to disrespect your father, do you?" Bull asked.

Layla sighed. "No. I don't. But I don't want you hovering over me."

"I promise not to hover," he said.

"Good, now I've really got to get going. My father has strict rules about being at dinner on time. Sometimes, we have guests, and he doesn't like to keep them waiting."

"Very well." He waved a hand toward the door. "Lead the way."

Bull had to hurry to keep up with her. He snagged his suitcase as he passed the secretary's desk, and they walked on to the elevator. They descended a floor, got out and walked down a long corridor.

"I have the last room on the end. Apparently, yours is beside mine. When I go to bed at night, I don't like to be disturbed. I don't get up in the morning until at least eight o'clock, and I don't like people to talk to me until I've had my first cup of coffee."

He tapped his heels together and popped a salute. "Yes, ma'am."

Her brow descended. "And I don't like when people patronize me."

He grinned. "Yes, ma'am."

"And you can't go around calling me ma'am if we're supposed to be engaged."

"Yes—" He paused. "What do you want me to call you? Do I have a pet name for you?"

She shook her head. "I've never had a pet name or nickname."

"Well, your given name is Layla. I could call you Layla or my pet name for you could be Lolli."

She rolled her eyes. "No, just no. Call me Layla. And I can't call you Mr. Smith."

He'd be hard pressed to answer to it anyway, since his last name wasn't Smith. "Well, my first name is Greg," he said. It was Craig, but she didn't need to know that. He was undercover, and it was close enough. Craig sounded enough like Greg, that he wouldn't get confused. "My friends call me Bull."

Layla frowned. "Don't your friends like you?"

He laughed. They called him Bull because his real last name was Bullington. For the duration of the assignment, his last name was Smith. He couldn't tell her about the true nature of his nickname being a derivative of his real last name. Instead, he waved a hand in front of him. "I'm so large, my friends call me Bull because they think I'm like a bull in a china shop.

She nodded with a smile. "I can see that."

"You can call me Greg, or you can call me Bull. I don't care."

She stared at him for a long moment. "I think I'll call you Bull. But not because of a bull in a china shop, but more because of the bullshit we're having to put up with." She grinned. "Yeah, I like it. I'm gonna call you Bull."

It didn't bother Bull. His friends had called him worse.

She walked toward her room. "I leave for dinner at fifteen minutes before the hour. If you plan to escort me down, be ready."

He nodded. "What's the uniform for the evening?"

She shook her head. "We have to work on that military speak. Dinner attire is formal. You'll need a black suit and tie."

Thank goodness he'd packed one. Now all he needed was an iron to get out all of the wrinkles.

Layla ducked into her room.

He entered his, tossed his suitcase up on the bed and rummaged through it to find the suit they'd come up with for the assignment. Thankfully they'd found one off the rack in a store downtown.

It wasn't a perfect fit, but it was close enough. The entire time he was getting ready, he listened for the sound of her door opening. If he was to keep her safe, he needed to be with her twenty-four-seven. Being one door away from her, was one door too many. But Bull was absolutely certain she would not agree to him sleeping in the same room as her. He'd have to make do and keep his ears open.

Fifteen minutes before the hour, he stepped out into the hallway.

Layla's door opened, and she emerged wearing a long black dress that hugged her from her breasts to her thighs and fell down in soft folds to her ankles. On her feet, she wore high heeled, strappy sandals sprinkled with shiny crystals. She'd swept her glorious dark hair up into a sleek arrangement at the back of her head with tiny tendrils of hair drifting down along her neck. Sparkly diamond hoops dangled from her ears, and a matching pendant nestled above her cleavage, held in place with a gold chain.

Bull's breath caught in his throat.

The woman was stunning. Dark, sultry and so beautiful, he could barely draw in a deep breath.

Her gaze raked over him, and she nodded with a small smile. "Not bad, for a soldier."

Bull silently thanked his mother for forcing him to train for and attend cotillion. He'd recognize the place settings and the numerous eating utensils beside the plates. At least, he wouldn't have to guess which one to use for what. He could practically guarantee that none of the other men on his team would know a salad fork from a prawn fork.

But his dinner partner…

Wow.

Bull prayed he didn't trip over his new dress shoes as he escorted her down the hallway to the elevator.

ABOUT THE AUTHOR

ELLE JAMES is a *New York Times* and *USA Today* Bestselling author of books including cowboys, intrigues and paranormal adventures that keep her readers on the edges of their seats. When she's not at her computer, she's traveling, snow skiing, boating, or riding her ATV, dreaming up new stories. Learn more about Elle James at www.ellejames.com

Website | Facebook | Twitter | GoodReads | Newsletter | BookBub | Amazon

Follow Me!
www.ellejames.com
ellejames@ellejames.com

ALSO BY ELLE JAMES

Simon (#8)

Maurice (#9)

Jacques (#10)

Brotherhood Protectors Yellowstone

Saving Kyla (#1)

Saving Chelsea (#2)

Saving Amanda (#3)

Saving Liliana (#4)

Saving Breely (#5)

Saving Savvie (#6)

Saving Jenna (#7)

Saving Peyton (#8)

Saving Londyn (#9)

Brotherhood Protectors Colorado

SEAL Salvation (#1)

Rocky Mountain Rescue (#2)

Ranger Redemption (#3)

Tactical Takeover (#4)

Colorado Conspiracy (#5)

Rocky Mountain Madness (#6)

Free Fall (#7)

Murdock (#8)

Utah (#9)

Judge (#10)

Delta Force Strong

Ivy's Delta (Delta Force 3 Crossover)

Breaking Silence (#1)

Breaking Rules (#2)

Breaking Away (#3)

Breaking Free (#4)

Breaking Hearts (#5)

Breaking Ties (#6)

Breaking Point (#7)

Breaking Dawn (#8)

Breaking Promises (#9)

Hearts & Heroes Series

Wyatt's War (#1)

Mack's Witness (#2)

Ronin's Return (#3)

Sam's Surrender (#4)

Hellfire Series

Hellfire, Texas (#1)

Love & War (#4)

Billionaire Online Dating Service

The Billionaire Husband Test (#1)

The Billionaire Cinderella Test (#2)

The Billionaire Bride Test (#3)

The Billionaire Daddy Test (#4)

The Billionaire Matchmaker Test (#5)

The Billionaire Glitch Date (#6)

The Billionaire Perfect Date (#7) coming soon

The Billionaire Replacement Date (#8) coming soon

The Billionaire Wedding Date (#9) coming soon

Cajun Magic Mystery Series

Voodoo on the Bayou (#1)

Voodoo for Two (#2)

Deja Voodoo (#3)

Cajun Magic Mysteries Books 1-3

The Outriders

Homicide at Whiskey Gulch (#1)

Hideout at Whiskey Gulch (#2)

Held Hostage at Whiskey Gulch (#3)

Setup at Whiskey Gulch (#4)

SEAL Of My Own

Navy SEAL Survival

Navy SEAL Captive

Navy SEAL To Die For

Navy SEAL Six Pack

Devil's Shroud Series

Deadly Reckoning (#1)

Deadly Engagement (#2)

Deadly Liaisons (#3)

Deadly Allure (#4)

Deadly Obsession (#5)

Deadly Fall (#6)

Covert Cowboys Inc Series

Triggered (#1)

Taking Aim (#2)

Bodyguard Under Fire (#3)

Cowboy Resurrected (#4)

Navy SEAL Justice (#5)

Navy SEAL Newlywed (#6)

High Country Hideout (#7)

Clandestine Christmas (#8)

Thunder Horse Series

Hostage to Thunder Horse (#1)

Thunder Horse Heritage (#2)

Thunder Horse Redemption (#3)

Christmas at Thunder Horse Ranch (#4)

Demon Series

Hot Demon Nights (#1)

Demon's Embrace (#2)

Tempting the Demon (#3)

Lords of the Underworld

Witch's Initiation (#1)

Witch's Seduction (#2)

The Witch's Desire (#3)

Possessing the Witch (#4)

Stealth Operations Specialists (SOS)

Nick of Time

Alaskan Fantasy

Boys Behaving Badly Anthologies

Rogues (#1)

Blue Collar (#2)

Baby Bling

Under Suspicion, With Child

Texas-Size Secrets

Cowboy Sanctuary

Lakota Baby

Dakota Meltdown

Beneath the Texas Moon